CLEANSING FIRES

A DCI GARRICK THRILLER - BOOK 5

M.G. COLE

GW00480900

TANGLEBOX
BOOKS

CLEANSING FIRES

A DCI Garrick mystery - Book 5

Copyright © 2022 by Max Cole (M.G.Cole)

Cover art: Shutterstock

1

_____

The radiating warmth erased the night-time chill. Not that the violent shivers coursing through Sajan Malik's body were his primary concern. The frost stung his bare feet until they had become numb from pounding across the frozen tarmac. The screech of rubber tyres and the wash of full-beam headlights warned the pursuing vehicle was close behind him.

He wasn't a fit man by any standards. Despite the numbness, he limped as the muscles in his right leg screamed in pain. He had just enough energy to lurch up the high kerb and onto the pavement as the vehicle sped past at speed. The rush of air propelled him forward, and he felt something swipe across his backside. It was only when he heard the tinkle of a breaking mirror and a hollow plastic clack, did he glance back to see the wing mirror that had clipped him was now bouncing across the flagstones. A deeper chill in his leg made him wonder if the impact had drawn blood.

The van had overshot him by a dozen yards. The brake lights blazed deep red as they locked hard, putting it into a controlled skid. The noise echoed around the empty industrial estate, and Sajan cursed his impulsive decision to come this way. Had he not fled across the dual carriageway, he would have been in the relative safety of his housing estate where he could have attracted help.

Out here he was on his own.

In the dim light offered by a waxing moon, he could make out the dark structures of a pair of shuttered industrial units, separated by the thick shadows of a narrow alleyway. Far too tight for the van to follow him down.

Sajan threw himself into the shadows. His frozen toes kicked fragments of metal, discarded parts that hid in the gloom. Glass crunched under his bare feet and moments later he slipped, probably on his own blood. Luckily, it was too dark for him to see what gruesome horrors his feet had turned into. Rushing onwards was the only choice he had.

He didn't see the chain-link fence stretching across his path until he ran into it at speed. The cold metal lattice bit into his forehead with an oddly soft blow, and he rebounded against the wall. The obstruction had taken the wind from him - but a quick glance behind showed his pursuer squealing to a halt. Movement across the headlights told him that the driver was now out of the vehicle and sprinting towards him.

Sajan contemplated climbing the fence. Against the sky, he could just see it stretch up a full ten feet. Perhaps a running jump at it...?

Then he saw a fire door in the wall opposite him, sunken into a recess to be almost invisible in the night. There were no latches or handles. The door was designed to be opened from just one direction, from the inside. He just prayed that the metal was corroded just enough to jar it open.

He grunted as he shouldered the door as hard as he could and was rewarded with the trickle of detritus from its surface. He thrust again. A clank of falling metal from inside gave him hope.

He shouldered it for a third time and heard the satisfying scrape of metal as the door popped open. He had hoped for an alarm, something to help draw attention to his plight, but he was rewarded with nothing more than the nearing foot-steps of his pursuer.

Sajan blindly groped for the edge of the door. He forced his fingers into the tiny gap and hauled it towards him. The door scraped against rubbish on the step, but he opened it wide enough to squeeze through. He fell to his knees inside the void beyond and crawled into the darkness. He just stopped himself from bumping into a steel shelving rack as his eyes adjusted to a dull red light, presumably activated when the fire door opened. He was in an aisle with racks either side. To the left were sacks, the light reflecting from their plastic covers. Some sort of metal spray cannisters lined the metal shelves, although it was too dim to make out details.

With a whimper of pain shooting through his leg, Sajan reached up and gripped the edge of the shelf. He shook violently as he hauled himself upright. His leg trembled as it took his weight. He was almost straight when something heavy connected with the back of his neck. Blackness strobed across his vision as he blinded in-and-out of consciousness before landing on his side, hard on the floor. A boot to his chest, so savage that he heard a rib crack, rolled him onto his back.

The figure towering over him had the substance of a

shadow. Only his laboured panting hinted at any suggestion of humanity.

"No more running, mate." The voice was low and deep, threaded with hideous menace. "Just so you know, tonight you die." It was a matter-of-fact statement. "But it's gonna be very slow."

Sajan opened his mouth to speak, but his mouth was too dry. Another swipe of the boot struck him across the face, knocking a tooth out. The figure crouched, lowering his voice even more.

"Now it's time to burn for your sins, mate."

Sajan thought he'd experienced pain before.

But he was wrong. Very wrong.

2

———————

"What a discovery. Could you imagine?"

The bones were tightly packed together, giving the promise of being identifiable without actually being so.

David Garrick leaned closer for a better view. He pointed, tracing the arcing vertebra. "Very clear spinal cord. Once you've found that, you know you have something very specific."

He sensed movement from behind as his companion craned close to his shoulder for a better look.

"And what would you say the cause of death was?"

Garrick shrugged. "Impossible to tell from these remains. He was big, though. Maybe... thirteen feet tall." He let out a low whistle and looked back to gauge Wendy's reaction. She pulled a face.

"I thought dinosaurs were bigger than that."

She reappraised the large, coiled skeleton behind the glass. Its bones laid out in the rock in which it was found.

"You're never impressed," Garrick said with a smile.

"Imagine finding this fossil on the beach. An iguanodon! Or as they now insist on calling it, a Mantellisaurus, after the bloke who found it."

"That's a... claim to fame," said Wendy in a tone that stated she'd never heard of the man before now. "And one day you hope you'll find a fossil on the beach, and it will end up here." She nodded towards the display case.

Garrick chuckled. "That's the dream. You know this is a fake, right?"

Wendy rolled her eyes and sighed theatrically. "Why, detective chief inspector, whatever do you mean?"

"It's a cast of the find. The original is in London's Natural History Museum."

"So you've dragged me to Maidstone to look at a fake?"

"Dragged is harsh," Garrick said, gesturing around. "Who ever thought Maidstone was synonymous with dinosaurs? They even commemorated it on a fifty pence piece recently."

"I'll have to check my small change," said Wendy, with an eye on the exit.

She was deliberately playing up. Over the last few months, she had secretly been delighted to have Garrick all to herself as he recovered from his operation. It had been a terrific excuse to visit some of the local Kentish tourist spots that locals never bothered with, and it was a welcome chance to spend some time away from their work.

Wendy twisted Garrick's wheelchair towards the exit in a clear sign they'd seen everything they'd intended. He didn't need the wheelchair, but for everyday out they'd had, Wendy had pre-booked one as a joke. At first, Garrick was visibly pissed-off, but he soon settled into the spirit of being pampered and turned the situation around by teasing Wendy that she was now merely a servant to the emperor. That would have ordinarily earned him a playful clip around the back of the head, but after his brain surgery, she refrained from violence. Only just.

As they strode out into the unseasonable sunshine, Garrick angled his black NY baseball cap. He'd never been to New York, and hats of any sort were something he thought never suited him, but in this case, it hid the circular bald patch on the side of his skull. A necessary war wound from his procedure that left an ugly red patch of skin. The scar would never go, but a forest of stubble had already sprouted, giving him hope that it would be concealed sooner than later.

On their stroll into the town centre, Garrick enjoyed the warmth of the sun on his face. Without thinking, he stopped and closed his eyes. It was a moment of mindfulness as the sounds of the idle conversation and constant traffic washed over him. Even surrounded by concrete and commerce, Garrick felt an overwhelming sense of being alive. His job always placed him in lockstep with death, especially the last year. The discovery of a growth on his brain and the resulting surgery had shaken him to the core, an unwelcome reminder of his own mortality. Coupled with the haunting spectre of his sister's murder...

Thinking of Emilie brought with it a tsunami of conflicting emotions – especially the last haunting vision he'd had as he'd slipped unconscious before surgery. She was there, in glorious technicolour, leaning over him and smiling. A hallucination, but a troubling one. Wendy's voice prickled his attention.

"Mmm?"

"I said, should we eat here?" She indicated to Nando's opposite.

Garrick shrugged. He had no problem with chicken but

was puzzled by the fuss surrounded a restaurant where you effectively had to serve yourself. Still, Wendy was keen on it.

They sat at the table and studied the menu. Or at least he did. Wendy had her specific favourite: the Chicken Butterfly. She was excited about the next steps they had decided in their relationship, as was Garrick. It was new, uncharted territory, and while he was effectively on sick leave from work, it was probably the right time, too.

He glanced at his phone as it buzzed. He'd missed a call from his office. He frowned, wondering who it was. There was a message, but he decided he'd listen to it after lunch. After all, there was no rush to get back.

Even if he hated the fact that he missed the challenges the job threw at him. It was, after all, part of what made his life worth living.

3

Max licked Garrick so hard across the face it felt like a warm slap. The spaniel was, by Garrick's limited knowledge of canine behaviour, wildly hyperactive. Yet his handler assured him that Max was exceptional. With a double-whistle, she had the dog peel away from Garrick and continue sniffing through the destruction.

The origin of the fire was clear from the pattern of destruction. The warehouse was one of fifteen in the industrial estate, and it had exploded with great intensity, fanning flames across the two adjoining units. High winds on the night had then driven the flames in a single direction, setting alight two more units and badly scorching the roof of a third before the fire engines arrived.

The unit housed volatile chemicals housed for an industrial cleaning company that had passed their last safety inspection with flying colours. Still, accidents happened. So did intentional destruction.

With the Kent Police Force stretched, Garrick had been lured back to work with the promise of 'easier' cases while he was still recovering from his operation. It wasn't ideal, and perhaps in more normal times he would've pushed his sick leave to the max. But even with Wendy to occupy him, Garrick found himself sinking into dark fugues when he was forced to spend time alone.

His illness and accompanying hallucinations – most of which he still hadn't dared tell the doctors about, his sister's death and the baggage of his ex-friend, John Howard, being revealed as a serial killer who had designed a personal psychological attack on Garrick himself – had all left its mark on his psyche.

While he had been off, Superintendent Margery Drury had been placed on gardening leave because of her closeness to Police Commissioner Scott Edwards, who Garrick had exposed to be part of a notorious 'Murder Club', created by Howard. The investigation, run by DCI Kane from the London Met, continued rolling forward, but it was deemed that Drury be allowed back to her position. Her first task was to convince Garrick to get back to work. It had taken two expensive meals at her golf course, and long conversations in which she told Garrick he was the only person she felt that she could trust.

He felt guilty that her trust was slightly misplaced. He was already willing to come back. The two fine meals just made it a sweeter deal. In addition, his doctor was pleased with how quickly he was recovering, and he was certain he wasn't having any more hallucinations caused by the growth pushing against his brain.

The violent flashbacks, however, were something else.

He found that he could be distracted or upbeat one moment, then the mutilated image of Dr Amy Harman seared unbidden in his mind's eye. She had been his psychiatrist and a victim of the Murder Club. She'd been carved up in his own home, left with a message scrawled in blood just to taunt him. Other than her connection to Garrick, she had been an innocent victim in an insidious game. He had seen many dead bodies over his career, yet the image of the attractive young woman would forever haunt him. Wavey blonde hair matted with her own blood. Lifeless blue eyes were open and staring straight at him. Every detail, the folds in her shirt, fingers clenched as they dug into the carpet as she endured the final throes of agony – it would all suddenly appear in his mind as vivid as the evening he'd found her. And the smell. The metallic scent of blood had filled the landing outside his bedroom. Even after completely redecorating the crime scene, it lingered. At least it did for him.

He hadn't returned for more than half an hour to retrieve clothes and toiletries. He'd spent time in the Maidstone Travel Inn, then in the hospital. After he was discharged, he returned to the cheap hotel. That was why Wendy had insisted that he move in with her so she could keep an eye on him.

Although it was a decision made in love, he couldn't shake the idea that it was a more practical step than a romantic one, and definitely not the way he had imagined their relationship would go. Somewhere along the way, he and Wendy had moved into a high gear without all the usual steps in between, but it had been the correct choice. Or if not correct, the sensible one. He decided not to tell anybody about the flashbacks as he had no desire to spend more time with another HR appointed shrink deciding whether or not he was fit for work.

"She's got a fix." The dog handler's voice barely cut above Garrick's inner monologue.

Garrick was embarrassed to realise that he had been staring into space, a bad habit he had recently developed. The little spaniel was whining and pawing at the charred ashes thirty feet away. The explosion had torn the roof from the building, exposing it to the cool winter air, but some of the metal supporting beams were still in place, blackened with ash and the heat from the fire. Garrick checked his fluorescent yellow hard hat was secure, then followed the dog handler. He couldn't hear the gentle commands issued to the dog, but they seemed to please the pooch, who barked and pressed himself around the handler's legs so he could enjoy a hearty belly rub for a job well done.

Garrick stared at the remains of the metal canister the dog had uncovered. It was no larger than a standard oil can, and any identifying markings had been removed by the heat.

"A possible accelerant," the handler stated, nodding at it. She rubbed the top of the dog's head. "Sammy here can pick out forty different types that you or I could never tell the difference between in a million years."

"Could it have been one of the chemicals stored here?"

The handler shrugged. "Unlikely, but they'll have an inventory we can check it against. Some chemicals shouldn't be stored together, and that can doesn't look like a secure one to me."

"So somebody has been arsin' around," Garrick said as he circled the offending object. He was mildly disappointed the handler hadn't acknowledged his pun, but guessed that she'd probably heard it endlessly. Out of the panoply of crimes, Garrick found arson one of the most unpalatable. While murder could be accidental, arson was completely premeditated, and its very nature meant it easily spiralled out of control, affecting more people than just the intended target. It was a blunt weapon used without discretion or thought of the consequences. A true sociopathic crime.

More barking from across the warehouse made him look up. Another dog, this one a black Labrador, was excitedly pawing at a pile of ashes.

"That's not good," came the soft Geordie accent of the Fire Investigation Officer behind Garrick. Jack Weaver was six-foot two of muscle, lean lines, and stubble. In Garrick's opinion, he was a walking stereotype of a firefighter and belonged more on the pages of a calendar than in a bright yellow fire jacket and hard hat.

The 'corpse dog', as he'd been introduced to Garrick, was specialised in detecting bodies. Or in this instance, victims. Already the ashes had been cleared enough to reveal a scorched bone. Garrick was too far away to see exactly what it was. He took a step – but felt Weaver's firm hand grip his shoulder and pull him back.

"Hold on," was all the investigator said. As Kent's Fire and Rescue Services' main investigator on this incident, he handled safety on site, including Garrick's. Then he suddenly bellowed, "Jo – back off now!"

Without missing a beat, the dog handler yanked the Labrador back, and they both sprinted towards Weaver. Just in time as the ceiling spar above them gave a low creak. Detritus trickled down – then seconds later one side of the bar gave way and swung to the ground where both man and dog had been. Garrick knew that he would have been kneeling at that very spot if Weaver's keen sixth sense hadn't detected something amiss.

A plume of ash turned the air grey, and the jarring noise had sent both dogs into a yapping frenzy. Even as the cloud dissipated, Garrick could see the bones had already been covered once again. He sighed at the symbolism – it was time for him to start digging and find out just who the victim was.

Despite the situation, Garrick struggled to contain a smile of relief. After everything he'd been through recently, it was good to be back.

4

Things change, mused Garrick as he entered the incident room in the Maidstone police station. The empty evidence board and six desks with sleeping computers connected to the secure intranet, all looked ready to use. The absence of his team was the only real difference, yet he couldn't shake the feeling that there was *something else* different. Something he couldn't put his finger on. It was in the atmosphere, in the grain of the building. Something was amiss.

"Is that the not-so gently clomping of size tens in my office?" Garrick spun around. Detective Constable Harry Lord flashed an irrepressible grin and rushed over to pump Garrick's hand. "Welcome back, Guv."

Garrick felt as if he had been staring intently at Harry's limp, but the DC did not indicate that he'd noticed. He had been told it was permanent after he'd bounced over the bonnet of a car while on duty. His five-a-side days were over because too much effort sent a searing pain up his thigh. Garrick took a shuddering breath as he thought about the personal sacrifices that he and his team had taken during their short time together. Lord misinterpreted his reaction and eased his grip.

"Getting soft in your old age," he quipped. "I couldn't believe it when the Super said you'd be back early. We've all been up in Ebbsfleet. Nicer food in the canteen, warmer too, but other than that, it's a soulless place."

DCI Kane had run his operation to track down the Murder Club from Ebbsfleet. Since the recent bout of arrests, he'd moved back to his office in the Met, and Garrick's team had been seconded to the more modern North Kent offices. He'd been a little worried that Drury wouldn't be able to release his team, but she had pulled a few strings.

"Cuppa?"

Garrick looked around with a frown. "I wasn't sure anybody would want to come back, to be honest."

"Are you kidding? I have to knacker up this other leg. I reckon if I limp on both, then nobody will notice."

"Stick with me and I bet we can get you a hip-replacement within the year."

Lord nodded, pretending to appreciate the thought. "Anyway, you know what it's like. All we've been doing is paperwork." He flashed a look that both men understood. Paperwork, the enemy of exciting police work. Essential, well, to a degree, but it mounted up to smothering degrees and swallowed valuable time that could be spent on active investigations rather than sewing up old ones. 'Case closed' was a phrase they only really heard in tacky television shows. There seemed to always be something left to do.

Garrick hadn't been told if *everybody* was returning. Before his operation, there had been tensions in the team, and DC Fanta Liu had been injured in the line of duty.

Combined with the fact that she was dating DC Sean Wilkes just added further gloom to the situation.

Then he had been rushed into surgery. A few days later, and it could've been too late. CTE was a phrase he remembered, but his exact condition kept slipping his mind. Wendy had done far more research into it than he cared to listen to. As far as he was concerned, it was over, but the resulting convalescence period meant a much-needed time of bonding and repair between his team hadn't occurred.

Lord broke his thoughts. "So, what's the latest?"

"Arson."

Harry Lord's mouth pursed to deliver a pun, but it withered when he caught Garrick's warning expression.

"A deceased on the scene," Garrick continued. "Still waiting for the lab. We've got to get the case set up on HOLMES." He nudged a mouse to wake the computer and was greeted by a password prompt. He typed it in his old one and was told that it had expired. "Brilliant. Can't even get into our own computers."

"Fanta normally sorts this stuff out," said Lord, moving purposefully towards the corridor and the shared kitchen beyond. "Cuppa?"

Garrick tried his password again, just in case he'd typed it incorrectly, but received the same message.

"Bugger," he said under his breath. He'd kept track of his team while on leave and had received various get-well-soon cards from them, but there had been no other communication other than from Harry Lord, and most of that was via WhatsApp. A couple of times Harry had threatened to visit him, but Garrick had given thin excuses because he hadn't wanted the company. He glanced up from the screen to see

Lord was eying him with a hint of concern. "Heard from Chib?"

DS Chibarameze Okon was a spanner in the works with the smooth running of his team. She was his right-hand woman, so it was essential that the others worked confidently with her. However, when it was revealed that Kane had inserted her in the team to monitor him, after his last detective sergeant had been seconded – and later murdered – while working for DCI Kane's operation, trust in his second had fractured.

Chib had proved to be one of the most competent officers he'd ever worked with. Worse, she'd saved his life on more than one occasion. That made her betrayal even more bitter. If betrayal it really was. After all, she was just doing her job. There was corruption within the force linked to the Murder Club, and with Garrick's own sister marked as a victim, it was prudent to monitor him and his team. It's what he would have done.

Throughout the intense experience they had all been put through, Chib had been torn between her duty to DCI Oliver Kane and Garrick. She had ultimately supported Garrick, which could have been potentially career damaging.

Since he had been through surgery, he hadn't heard from her. Not even a card.

Harry Lord cleared his throat. "She went back to London with Kane. She came to Ebbsfleet a couple of times..." He let the sentence hang. Garrick couldn't tell if she had been shunned, or if the atmosphere had been difficult. "I'll get that cuppa going then." Lord quickly exited before Garrick could painfully drag the conversation out.

. . .

IT TOOK ALMOST two hours for a technician to reset Garrick's access passwords, and he was treated to the usual surliness that whiz kids seemed to bestow on those who knew less than them. Which was most people they encountered.

Crowded around the same computer, it took him and DC Harry Lord another wasted thirty minutes setting up the new investigation on the police HOLMES system. Harry's comment that they perhaps needed to attend a refresher training program sent chills through Garrick as his emails came through from Jack Weaver with various fire department reports and the initial findings from the forensic team. Harry had sent through the relevant pages to the printer when a visitor caught their attention.

"Why does it look like you two are playing a game rather than doing any serious sleuthing?"

Garrick sprung to his feet when DC Fanta Liu entered the room. He crossed to her and extended his hand – only for her to embrace him in a crushing hug that squeezed the breath from him.

"Great to see you alive, Dave!" She was much shorter than he was, so her muffled voice came from somewhere around his armpit.

"You too, Pepsi."

Neither moved for a moment, before Garrick became aware how awkward this could look to a passer-by. She had already thanked him for saving her life when she walked into a booby trap at a suspect's house. Garrick still felt a deep sense of guilt that she wouldn't have been in the situation if he hadn't operated 'off the book' and broke into the house in the first place. The spectre of facing a disciplinary tribune for breaking the rules still hadn't disappeared, but as it was connected to exposing serial killers and police corruption, it was a delicate situation. Nobody was currently willing to paint DCI David Garrick in a bad light.

He gently shoved Fanta away and forced his smile back to a more sombre look. "Good to have you back, DC Liu. And that's the last time I'll hear Dave in this office."

She raised a thin eyebrow in defiance, but said nothing. Garrick couldn't help but notice the faint scar running from her left eye, up across her forehead, to under the scalp. She had triggered the booby trap when she opened the door, detonating a gas canister. The door had saved her from severe injury. Had she been any swifter entering the room, fragments from the exploding cylinder could have diced her apart. Instead, the remarkably sturdy door had been blown off its hinges and acted as a shield. The detonation had destroyed the exterior wall and the staircase landing that Fanta had been standing on. She had dropped several feet to the ground and cracked her head against the door, knocking her out. The thick wood had protected her from falling masonry.

Garrick indicated her desk. "And just in time. DC Lord was about to make one of his infamous brews, and you're just in time to add the forensic reports from our new case."

Fanta gave a mock salute and dropped into her swivel chair with so much gusto that it rolled a foot to the side before she could stop herself. "Aye, aye!"

As Lord left for the kitchen, Garrick took a moment to enjoy the soft clack of Fanta's typing, and the distant faint sounds of ringing phone from other offices further down the corridor. The air was chilly, he still hadn't taken his coat off, and there was a perpetual stale smell to the air because of the building's age and dwindling maintenance – yet it felt familiar. More of a home than his own.

He quickly ushered away the thought that he was becoming a slave to work. It may be true, but it was also the last toehold he had in his old life. Everything else had irrevocably changed, and he wasn't entirely sure how he felt about that.

It wasn't until Lord had returned and distributed the drinks did Garrick speak up again. "Any word on the others?"

Fanta looked up, knowing the question was directed solely at her.

"Sean has to stay in Ebbsfleet for another couple of days." She blinked as Garrick looked at her expectantly. "And..." She shrugged, unsure what else was expected. Then she suddenly understood. "Oh! Chib? Dunno. But if you need a DS..." she indicated to herself.

"Nice try."

With two members of his team missing and no other support officers assigned to his case, Garrick suspected that the investigation was going to be a slow one. Drury had assigned it to ease him back into work, so he didn't think it would be a particularly taxing case, but he didn't want to make his boss think that he could get by with fewer resources, either.

A text from Wendy pulled his attention away from the room. She was asking what he wanted to eat tonight. The problem was that she was an average cook, and he was utterly terrible. His bachelor life had been sustained almost entirely on microwavable food. He was still finding it odd to eat with another person at home. The routines he had built over the years, such as not placing the food on a plate, but eating straight out of the plastic container, eating in front of the TV, and occasionally having the dessert first, had all been thrown to the wind. Wendy insisted on a more disciplined meal structure at a real dining table. As they bounced texts back and forth, he mused how easily he had succumbed to her way of doing things. Most of the bad habits that had been erased were his; not that she didn't have some of her own, but they weren't something that bothered him for more than a fleeting moment. Did that mean he was more tolerant? Or was she intolerant, forcing him to change so many of his foibles?

Or was he already over-thinking their relationship?

"Guv?"

Lord's voice pulled him back into the room. His two DCs had been busy setting up the evidence board with a map and photo of the industrial estate. As was usual with the start of most cases, the board was mostly empty. The words VICTIM and OWNERS written either side of it. The fire brigade inspection unit had its own little box in the corner, noting an accelerant was used. Under *property owners,* Fanta had added a list of points they needed to look at, which basically boiled down to checking that this wasn't an insurance fraud that had gone wrong. She'd added a few pound symbols for emphasis, making them so bold that Garrick could smell the marker ink from halfway across the room.

"I take it you think this is a crime about cash?" he said.

"Always follow the money." Fanta tapped the board for emphasis. "My gut is telling me that's exactly what this is about. Look at the scale of the damage. The report said three engines were called out to stop the flames. Somebody's hiding something."

Garrick nodded in agreement. It was the easiest excuse, with the poor victim being in the wrong place at the wrong time. A short, dry laugh from Lord made him suddenly doubt that assumption.

"I think your guts a little off, Liu." Harry Lord was scrolling through an email on the screen. "We have a DNA match on the victim."

Garrick and Fanta exchanged a look as he lapsed into an irritating silence as he read.

"And...?" Garrick prompted.

"And I think this may be a bit more involved than you think..." Harry said without taking his eyes off the screen.

5

Litter clattered across Garrick's feet as Fanta took a corner so fast that a discarded coke can bounced off his shin. The Polo's exhaust screamed with an unhealthy high note that Fanta had assured him was an intentional 'feature' after Sean had pimped the vehicle up. He couldn't work out why on earth anybody would want their car to sound so ill? However, his concern over her driving was reduced to his white-knuckle grip on the handle above the door. Annoyingly, she was a terrific driver, and her gusto just went to prove that she was back to her usual self.

"You know Harry gets wound up when he's left behind," she said as she glanced at the satnav on her phone, which was balanced against the radio's touchscreen. Even the briefest look caused her to over-compensate turning the wheel and Garrick felt his grip tighten as they veered towards the kerb. She jinked the wheel a second later.

Garrick found his voice. "When I go out with Harry, bad things seem to happen."

"Yeah. It's always a walk in the park when it's just us."

Dead bodies and exploding houses were already indelibly linked to Fanta's short career.

"You nagged me for fieldwork experience, DC Liu. Have you changed your mind?"

Fanta fell silent. Garrick thought she was concentrating on the road, but a quick glance and he saw her brow furrowed thoughtfully. After several moments, she spoke in an unusually quiet voice.

"No, sir." Her sudden unprovoked decorum rang alarm bells in Garrick's head. "It's just we're going to the coroner and, if I'm honest, it's not a part of the job I look forward to the most."

Garrick understood her reluctance. It had taken a large part of his career not to be repulsed by death. Each case had chipped away his revulsion and increased the dry gallows humour that kept coppers sane until he could view even the most gruesome crime scene through the eyes of a detached observer. It was only when he had to delve into the personal life of a victim did the emotions cry out that the victim was a real person, with real hopes and dreams.

"It's part of the job," he muttered with more coolness than he intended. DC Fanta Liu shifted position in her seat and didn't reply. Garrick felt an unexpected trickle of guilt. Was he being too harsh? Or had his recent convalescence softened him? He searched for a change of subject. "How did you find Ebbsfleet?"

Fanta gave a sharp sigh. "Boring. Filing and paperwork every day. Aren't we supposed to have support staff for that?"

"Lack of resources." Garrick was parroting an email from Drury that had warned the department was facing a budget review. In the light of recent events with Police Commissioner Scott Edwards' ties with the Murder Club, it wouldn't make the department shine. Combined with the Commissioner's homosexual relationship with John Howard – and that Garrick had been responsible for the man's accidental death – added a further awkward element to the whole mess. Drury had hinted that the powers that be wanted a fresh change of guard, which not only included Drury, but the man who had exposed the whole insidious affair. Garrick may be considered a hero, but that raised the question of how deep a mess were the Kent Constabulary in if they *needed* heroes.

"I missed good old detecting," Fanta continued. "What about you?"

"Mmm?" Once again, Garrick realised he had tuned out and focused on his own inner monologue.

"How was sick leave?"

"Oh, y'know... having somebody drill into your skull isn't as much fun as it sounds."

"Trepanning."

"What?"

"They used to call it trepanning. Doctors would drill into people's heads to relieve symptoms, like headaches."

"That sounds extreme." He could see Fanta was searching for the best way to phrase her question. He guessed what it was, so jumped straight in. "CTE. Chronic traumatic encephalopathy." She shot him a look. "You want to know what was wrong with me, right?" His unit had been given his medical reports when he had been investigated over Amy Harmon's death. He had later found out that Kane had at least been tactful enough not to give them every detail.

"It can be caused by too many traumas to the head. Like the ones a rugby player may suffer. Or in my case, every bloody case I seem to be on. It builds up a protein called tau around blood vessels and, well, in my case, can lead to swelling of the old noggin." He lightly tapped his hat, which covered the scar. Wendy had delved into the horrors that CTE can create, but he hadn't paid attention. He'd also been told it was inoperable, but his surgeons had put that idea to bed.

"So you're fine now?"

"I'm not going to start headbutting suspects, but I'm walking and talking, so it can't all be that bad. I look alright, don't I?"

"You look about the same."

He caught the flicker of a smile and knew she was deliberately being vague just to wind him up. That confirmed it for him – out of the two of them, Fanta was most definitely the one back on track.

THE USUAL SENSE of detachment that accompanied Garrick when visiting a mortuary had abandoned him today and he felt himself shiver as he and Fanta walked down the short corridor, the white walls seeing to gleam with extra brightness that hurt his eyes and forced him to squint. He tried to focus on the elderly coroner beside him, whose voice was so low that Garrick had trouble hearing a complete sentence. Fanta was two paces behind and unusually quiet.

They entered a small preparation room which was just as brightly lit, with a large circular halogen light above the central stainless-steel table. Garrick touched his ear as he could swear the light was emitting a high-pitch squeal, but the other two seemed oblivious to it. He forced himself to focus on the coroner's words.

"... Most of this, as you know."

Garrick scrambled to recall the beginning of the sentence.

He nodded and mumbled in agreement, hoping he hadn't agreed to anything. He looked at Fanta to see how she was holding up. Her unblinking gaze was fixed on the table. She'd seen dead bodies before, but it wasn't until he focused on the victim did, he understand *why*. The white sheet covering the cadaver showed only a bulge in the middle that was far too small for a person, even a child.

The coroner took off his round spectacles and buffed the lens on the tip of his white medical coat. "Fire plays havoc with a body, as I'm sure you can imagine." He replaced his glasses and moved to the edge of the sheet. "Then, with the roof collapsing, it added further... complications."

He slowly folded the sheet off the remains. Garrick had seen the hand the canine found, but seeing the rest of the body as a whole was unexpected. There was a head, torso, and the right arm. The pelvis was crushed and where the legs should be was just a mass of bone shards. He'd seen skeletal remains before, but this was something different.

The mass was covered with stretched black material. Like an optical illusion, it took Garrick several moments to understand that most of it was charred clothing that had melted under the heat, probably an acrylic waterproof jacket. Yet the hands and head were similarly tarnished. This was patchy skin that had turned as black as a forgotten Sunday roast. It had an unnaturally smooth, almost plastic, texture. Similarly, the hand and fingers looked as if they were tightly wrapped in a melted bin bag. The heat had fused the little and index finger together.

Details suddenly came into focus. Across the face, the skin was stretched to breaking point, the bone beneath was as black as charcoal. He was surprised to see patches of stubbled hair had survived the inferno.

Then there was the smell. The faint, but lingering scent of grilled pork. It was enough to put Garrick off barbeques for life. Or at least for a couple of weeks. He glanced at Fanta, who had paled considerably.

"That's a person?" her voice came as a croak.

The coroner's demeanour brightened as he sensed the opportunity for a lecture.

"The falling roof severed the left arm, and his legs were blown off by an explosion, which we think destroyed the arm." He circled the table, pointing to the remains' various parts. "Falling roofing joists shattered the pelvis while he was still alive. Skin usually burns at 162 degrees, so the skin you see is unusual." He peered over the rims of his spectacles. "I'm sure the fire department will have more to say on the thermodynamics of the warehouse and the type of accelerant used."

"Accelerant?" It was the first word Fanta had said with a clear voice.

"Arsonists use them to make sure things burn fast and furious," Garrick said. "And it can make extinguishing the blaze a lot more difficult."

The coroner nodded. "And sometimes, it can react with flesh, ironically preserving it to some degree, while the fat and muscle underneath essentially melts away."

Garrick frowned thoughtfully. "What actually killed him?"

The coroner indicated to the forearm. Now he was looking, Garrick could see it was buckled at a slight angle midway along the bone.

"This is possibly a defensive wound. Difficult to say for sure with no fleshy tissue to analyse, but it is in line with a heavy blunt object. A baseball bat, crowbar, that sort of thing.

This here," he indicated an indentation on the skull, just above what remained of the left ear, "looks to me like another blow to the head."

"Couldn't that be caused by the falling ceiling?" Fanta said, her confidence slowly returning.

The coroner pursed his lips as he thought. "This side of the head was against the floor and the photographs from the scene show the beams stopped short of striking his head, just his pelvis. My opinion is that he was struck at least twice. Doused in an accelerant and left dazed, possibly bleeding, but alive, as the fire was set."

"Burned alive," Garrick said softly.

The coroner nodded. "A hideous way to go, out of a long list of hideous deaths. The nervous system would still be firing, even as the surrounding flesh was destroyed. Every pain receptor triggering at the same time..."

Garrick shivered at the thought. "How was he identified?"

"Dental records. His attacker didn't try to destroy them. There was even a wallet in the remains of the jacket with credit cards inside. Unfortunately, everything had been fused together or completely melted, so they were useless." The coroner studied the remains, more with curiosity than disgust. "In my experience, it was certainly clear that the killer wanted him to suffer."

WALKING BACK TO THE CAR, both Fanta and Garrick sucked in lungfuls of cool afternoon air. Garrick hoped it would help get rid of the meaty smell that still permeated his nostrils. Fanta unlocked her car, but made no move to enter. Instead, she leaned on the roof and closed her eyes.

"It's never pleasant," Garrick assured her. "You did well in there."

"What a horrible way to die."

"I can't think of a good one."

"Drowning in chocolate?"

"Death by chocolate might not be as pleasant as you imagine. So, what do you make of it?"

"Totally a revenge killing," Fanta said, peering at her boss over the Polo's roof.

They'd had a head start in that department. Almost as soon as the body had been identified, DC Lord had located the man's criminal record. Sajan Malik. A 37-year-old British-Indian from Leicester, who had been living in Rochester for the last five years. He had been arrested twice for assaulting elderly women. Charges had been dropped the first time because of insufficient evidence, but a second attack in the woman's own home had seen him released on bail while he awaited a court date.

"And how would you go about the next step?"

Fanta opened the driver's door. The colour had returned to her cheeks, along with her determination.

"Speak to the families of his victims. I reckon somebody may be carrying a guilty conscience."

She slid into the driver's seat and slammed her door shut.

Garrick nodded, pleased with her assessment. However, he couldn't shake the feeling that something wasn't quite right with Fanta. Was she ready to work back in the field after her last experience? Or was he projecting fears for himself upon her?

Either way, something was amiss.

6

The roar from the blue flames made him flinch, which was definitely a sign that he was on edge.

"You look distracted."

The flame from the gas hob rippled hypnotically with flecks of orange. Garrick blinked and treated Wendy with a bemused smile.

"Still feeling a little tired." It wasn't a lie. Since the operation, he hadn't felt as if he was running on all cylinders. Most of that he put down to the physical marathon he'd endured, but he suspected part of it resulted from his new domestic situation. Natural small talk that couples developed over several long-term relationships was unfamiliar territory for him. He'd left the station promptly at 5 pm, with Harry Lord and Fanta Liu staying on for an extra hour to arrange interviews for the next day. He'd promised Wendy that he wouldn't immerse himself in casework unless he absolutely couldn't help it. His last venture, a kidnapping, had been so time critical that he was sure the pressure had accelerated his illness. He groped for a conversational thread. "How was work?"

Wendy rolled her eyes. "We have a parents' evening at the end of the week. A Friday. Who wants to spend extra time in school on a Friday? Not the parents, that's for sure. And of course all prep has been put onto the teaching assistants." She used both hands to indicate herself. "Three of us are expected to make sure everything runs smoothly."

Garrick grinned as her rant increased. He loved the way her nose scrunched and brow knitted when she imitated the staff members she didn't like; it was comical. Even her vocal impressions were worthy of Sesame Street. As he followed her into the living room as she continued describing her day, the awareness that there was nothing of his own decorating the room came crashing down around him. It was firmly still stamped with Wendy's personality. His fossil collection remained at his own house, with only his laptop migrating over and that was neatly tucked under the living room table next to a DVD boxed set of *Broadhaven* that he was dismayed to see hadn't made it to the charity shop. Perhaps that's why he was still feeling like a visitor here, more than a resident. Wendy sat on the sofa, and he sat on the arm, looming over her.

He slowly became aware of a long encroaching silence and realised Wendy had stopped talking and was looking at him oddly. He vaguely recalled her talking about quitting her job.

"Good idea," he said impulsively. Obviously, it wasn't the expected answer as she frowned.

"You zoned out, didn't you?"

"No, no. If you're unhappy with work, why not find something else?" He was improvising, but confident he'd picked up the correct conversational reins.

"With your house situation...?"

A quick change of mental gears. They'd spoken several times about Garrick selling his house. He had no desire to return there, and now living with Wendy had meant he wouldn't be homeless, even if she was renting. Despite the horrors that had occurred in his own home, it was still a big step for Garrick. A point of no return.

"I should speak to a couple of estate agents..." he mumbled.

Wendy let out a little sigh. "I mean, if I left my job and found nothing straight away, the rent here will be a struggle."

If he sold his house, he could easily cover it for a while. Garrick had never been money focused. As a child in Liverpool, his parents didn't have any, and his own salary was enough to get by without exotic holidays and luxury brands. He didn't consider himself a mean or frugal person, but the thought that he would be responsible for the both of them gave him pause for thought. Admittedly, he'd have to rent *somewhere* if he sold his house... but...

"Let's talk about this another time." Wendy smiled, but there was a touch of frost in her tone.

"No. Now is fine. I'm just..." he waved a hand in a circle as he searched for the right phrase.

"Out of it?"

"First proper day back and I'm running on deflated tyres." He hated the analogy, but at least it got his point across.

"You've been like this for a while." Wendy's lips tightened as if to stop her saying anything more incriminating. "I mean, out of sorts. Distracted. The doctor told you to track your moods."

"I feel fine. I'll get back up to speed. The incident today was a little unpleasant, so that's probably why."

When moving in, they had agreed that he wouldn't discuss anything about his cases. Of course, information was strictly classified, but even the subtlest hint could generate the most awkward atmosphere at home. Since Wendy had been partially dragged into his last escapade, she had no desire to ever repeat the experience.

She nodded, but not with belief. "Are you sure there is nothing else on your mind?"

Garrick kissed the top of her head and smiled. "Such as?"

"You talk in your sleep." That was news to Garrick. How long had he been doing that? Wendy studied his face. "Almost every night."

"What about?"

"Emelie is mentioned quite a lot."

Garrick's stomach churned. His nights had comprised dreamless slumber – or so he thought. The mention of his sister's name sent goose pimples along his arms.

The investigation into her death was still ongoing in the States and was now tied to DCI Kane's investigation here. While the body of her fiancé and several others had been found, all victims of the sickening Murder Club, hers was still missing. John Howard had been one of the key figures in the group and had targeted Emilie, seemingly as part of a larger plan to torment Garrick. And it had worked. Disturbing items had been sent to him – such as an empty envelope from America that had been sealed with her saliva. Phone messages created to imply that she was still alive. Even the gift of an expensive car that had turned up in his driveway, paid for with criminal funds in a bizarre attempt to implicate him in the murder cult. Every incident gnawed Garrick's psyche to the point where he had even hallucinated seeing his sister as the nurse pushing him into the operation theatre. He had been so dazed, confused, and frightened that he hadn't dared mention that to anybody. He was convinced that with the murderous cohort now exposed and dismantled, the stress would disappear.

Now it seemed he was wrong.

"What did I say?"

Wendy forced a thin smile. "You were tossing and turning. Mumbling. I only really caught her name. Every time I calmed you down, you'd slip into a deep, snore-filled sleep."

"Oh my God! I snore, too?" Garrick seized the opportunity to lighten the mood and forced a jovial laugh. It had the desired effect, and Wendy chuckled.

"Sometimes. Like a freight train."

He stood up in mock offense. "Oh? That must be to disguise the soundtrack of your stealth farts under the duvet."

"I do not!" Wendy barked, trying to hide a guilty smile.

They both laughed and kissed. The power of juvenile humour is grossly overlooked, Garrick thought as he headed back to the kitchen to see if the pasta had cooked. Out of sight from Wendy, he struggled to maintain the smile. He just needed his old focus back; control of his own thoughts and emotions. He hoped being back on a case would be the catharsis he needed.

He stopped and stared at the gas cooker. The burner was on full blast, but the pan of pasta and water was still on the draining board. He'd forgotten to cook. Garrick hoped that even the most basic tasks were not slipping away from him.

. . .

IN AN ATTEMPT not to appear bias, and following Fanta's discomfort yesterday, Garrick began the day's interviews accompanied by DC Harry Lord, who was in a boisterous mood and cracking jokes since Garrick had sat in the car. Garrick still felt guilty for stealing Harry's BMW, but the subject hadn't been mentioned since the unit had reformed. He suspected that Harry was happy enough to be out of Ebbsfleet.

Fanta wasn't thrilled about being left in the office, but with no sign of Chib, Sean, or any support staff, there was little choice. Plus, Garrick secretly thought she was a much better organiser than Harry. They didn't discuss the case at all. Instead, Garrick was happy to listen to a rambling conversation that drifted between last night's Arsenal footie match and several risqué jokes that he was pleased Harry didn't belch across the office. The lack of personal questions was a welcome relief and made the trip to the outskirts of Ramsgate a pleasant one.

Phyllis Carlisle was 74 and living with her daughter since the incident with Malik. She had been living alone in a bungalow for two years after her husband died when Malik had broken in through the rear bathroom window. He had shoved her to the floor and kicked several times, breaking three ribs. Malik hadn't stopped until he noticed she'd pulled a red emergency cord in the hallway as she'd fallen. The on-call advisor on the other end heard everything and called the police while shouting down the intruder from halfway across the country. Malik had fled, but been ID'd on two home security cameras several streets away.

Phyllis sat on a sofa next to her son-in-law, Danny. His t-shirt was a size too small, showing off his impressive muscular, tattooed biceps. His expression had been grim since the detectives had arrived. He did not try to make them feel welcome and showed a flicker of relief when Phyllis asked if anybody would like a cup of tea, and Garrick and Harry had politely declined. Garrick couldn't work out if Danny was just being protective, or if he had his own reasons for not trusting cops.

Garrick cleared his throat and regretted not accepting the drink. "As the detective told you on the phone, we are following up an incident with Mr Malik." Even though it had been almost two months since the encounter, he saw Phyllis tense at the mere mention of his name. Because of a backlog in cases, she still hadn't had her day in court. "I take it there has been no contact with him." That would've flagrantly violated his bail conditions and would have seen him straight behind bars.

Phyllis shook her head. "Not at all. What sort of incident? Has he done it again?"

"He was assaulted." Garrick didn't want to give too many details away at this stage.

Danny sniggered. "Nothing mild, I hope."

Garrick regarded him for a moment. "Enough to warrant police involvement," he finally said. "So you understand we have to look into everybody who may have issues with him."

Phyllis met Danny's eyes in a silent warning to shut up. "When was this?"

"The night before last."

A trace of a smile tugged the corner of Phyllis's mouth. "I was at bingo then. My daughter took me and picked me up."

Garrick chuckled good-naturedly. "That's good to know, Mrs Carlisle." She shifted his unblinking gaze onto Danny. "And you?"

"Busy."

Harry couldn't contain himself. "Bingo?"

"After what that piece of shit did to her, no pounding would be enough."

"You can never break too many bones, eh?" Harry had cemented his opinion on the man.

"Not with dickheads like that."

"Can you account for your movements over the last two days?" Garrick asked as casually as he could. "Just so we can eliminate you from our enquiries."

"I was here."

"And your wife will confirm that?"

Danny shrugged.

Garrick turned his attention back to Phyllis. "I appreciate how traumatic your incident was, and obviously people will naturally react with anger." He gestured to Danny. "And it's understandable that family are protective. Can you think of anybody you've spoken to who appeared overly angry?" He immediately regretted his choice of words.

Phyllis raised an eyebrow in surprise. "Overly angry that he broke into my home? Kicked me." She subconsciously touched her ribs. "I couldn't live on my own after that. Not after my Frank died…" Her voice cracked, but she quickly recovered. "He stole what little independence I had left. In my last years, I have become a burden to my family having to live here. It's difficult for me to go anywhere by myself." She raised her head, the frail elderly woman suddenly looking imperious. Garrick caught a hint of how powerful she once would have been. "I wish we still had the death penalty in this country, detective. People like him don't deserve forgiveness. They deserve every bad thing that comes to them."

7

"That's our prime suspect right there," Harry said, thumping the steering wheel with the palm of his hand.

"That's known as profiling," said Garrick.

Harry sucked in his breath. "That's a loaded word, but it doesn't mean it's all wrong." He was referring to the use of racial profiling, which was still a problem across the force. "I mean, a bunch of skinheaded Millwall supporters walk into a bar... what d'you think is gonna happen?"

"Wasn't that back in the eighties? The F-troop, I think they called them. Things change."

"Not always."

Both he and Harry had years of wearing down shoe leather on patrol before they became detectives. Harry took every opportunity to revel in his stories – always the most violent or gruesome ones – and treated them as a badge of honour. Garrick was thankful for moving away from the frontline. Detective work was usually safer and more predictable, although it hadn't been for the last year or so.

"We'll check up on his movements," Garrick said. "But I bet a pint he's more gas than action."

After a thoughtful silence, Harry added. "Although you can't blame him for being protective."

Garrick typed an email to update Fanta. "Sure. But there's a world away from a well-deserved thrashing compared to torture."

Harry grinned. "You missed your calling as a judge." He checked the GPS as they headed towards Malik's other victim, who lived in a nursing home in Broadstairs. This old dear was mugged in the street and couldn't offer an accurate description of his attacker. It was only after Malik was arrested for assaulting Phyllis Carlisle did officers find he'd kept the woman's purse, complete with cash card. As she had no family, they didn't think there would be any connection to Malik's killer.

Garrick sent the update to Fanta and noticed an email in his inbox from the fire investigator, who had some new updates. He considered calling him, but changed his mind and decided he'd head over there after lunch. The thought of being cooped up in the office wasn't appealing.

THE HEADQUARTERS for Kent's Fire and Rescue Service was in Tovil, just south of Maidstone. Jack Weaver greeted him a tiny office that barely seemed to contain him. The man's navy-blue polo shirt couldn't contain his muscular physique. Without looking, Garrick sensed Fanta brighten as she laid eyes on the man, who looked as if he'd just walked off a fashion shoot.

Garrick had thought it only fair to let her out of the office in the afternoon, and only belatedly had second thoughts on surrounding Fanta with muscular firemen. It had been a text from Wendy who'd triggered him when she pointed out how much she liked men in uniform. The playful flirting made him regret his troubled thoughts from the previous evening, and he mused how he could make more of an effort with her.

"Detective Garrick." Jack's firm grip crushed Garrick's hand.

"Mr Weaver–"

"Jack."

"Jack. This is DC Liu."

"Fanta," she replied, shaking his hand in return.

Garrick bit his tongue. So much for maintain an aura of professional detachment.

Jack indicated to the seats across from his desk. "Sit, please. Can I get you something to drink?" He glanced at a yellowing plastic kettle in the corner of his office.

"We're good."

Jack's swivel chair wheezed as he plopped his weight down on it. "I'm glad you came. It's so much easier to talk things through in person, rather than bounce emails all the time. We can get into a proper cut and thrust of the investigation," he added enthusiastically.

"I completely agree," said Garrick.

"It's always better in the flesh," Fanta said with a smile. Garrick felt like kicking her under the table, but stopped himself.

Jack quickly typed a password on his computer, then angled the screen so they could see. He had several images of the warehouse up, all slightly overlapping.

"This warehouse fire in Snodland is intriguing."

Garrick studied the pictures, but the mangled mass of burned support beams and ash offered no clues to him.

Jack consulted his notes. "It is owned by Ryland Cleaning Supplies. A privately owned company with units in Kent, Sussex, Surrey, and Berkshire. They sell cleaning products wholesale to whoever needs them."

"I suppose the warehouse was packed with them?"

"They'd had a delivery that very morning. There are a lot of regulations when it comes to the safe storage of chemicals. The Health and Safety Executive is very strict about what can and cannot be stored together, and what safety precautions must be in place."

"Because these things can blow up if mixed?" said Fanta. Garrick was pleased that she was at least making notes on her phone.

Jack gave a dry chuckle. "If we're lucky, that's all they'll do. To give you an example, bleach and vinegar can create chlorine gas, which is lethal." He rolled the mouse over several windows he had opened, then double-clicked a file. "This is the last HSE inspection report from two months ago. They passed, pending the alarm being fixed."

"So it was obviously accidental," Garrick clarified.

"In my opinion, it was good luck — from the arsonist's point of view — that they both ended up here. We've been working the forensics lab on what happened outside the warehouse. My job is to figure out how the blaze started and developed. We have an interesting picture."

He called up photographs of the exterior. The top of the warehouse was black and ragged from where the roof had blown off. Further down, towards the door, the brickwork was heavily smoke damaged. Only the bottom few feet looked untouched, although the shuttered entrance was raised by two feet, and the rest of it had been torn apart from the explosion, leaving only a ragged metal frame. He indicated to the alley at the side of the building. The adjacent unit was scorched black.

"The victim was chased up this alley, which is blocked at the end by a fence. Midway along is the fire door." He swapped images to show the closed door. Ironically, the blaze had left it untouched. "It was closed, but surviving DNA traces on the exterior show the victim entered this way. My best guess is his killer *didn't* exit this way."

"Why didn't the alarm go off?"

Jack's eyebrows raised in agreement. "The security alarm had been faulty for several months. The owners say they hadn't got around to repairing it."

"The victim was assaulted; we assume while inside. If he had to force a heavy fire door to get in, then that suggests he wasn't too badly injured when he broke in."

Jack nodded. "Unfortunately, any bloodstains or organic evidence would have been destroyed as temperatures soared. So we're relying on speculation."

"So that doesn't give us much to go on," said Fanta. "We have no video footage from any of the other units." She pulled a face.

"True. But that's where somebody like me comes in." He flashed a smile that made Fanta automatically respond with her own. "The first thing I need to establish is the seat of the fire." He caught Fanta's questioning look. "Where it started. That's very difficult when the fire itself can destroy all traces of its origin. Luckily, the shelving inside the warehouse was steel. And the melting point of that is roughly fourteen hundred Celsius. The blaze inside the warehouse reached an average of approximately six hundred degrees, which is enough to warp metal."

He showed them a plan of the warehouse with the shelves marked in neat lines, and the position of the corpse was indicated by a red dot.

"Based on the various warping of the shelves, I came up with this radius of error."

A yellow circle appeared over the image, with its centre two metres away from the body, next to a rack of shelves in the middle of the room.

"Now it was the north-east side of the roof that suffered complete damage. There were still panels remaining in the opposite corner. So an explosion from inside would have shot straight up, puncturing the roof. We found twenty-five burnt metal containers outside, four hundred yards away, near the trees. It looks as if they were the first to pop and shot straight up. With a hole in the ceiling, the flames would be supplied with a huge breath of oxygen." He revolved his hands around one another to simulate the air moving down. "Which would've accelerated the fire. Which in turn would have grown hotter—"

"And detonated more of the stock," Garrick finished in a thoughtful tone.

"It would've fanned the flames and increased the temperature to about seven hundred and fifty degrees, or thereabouts. That's the auto-ignition temperature for a lot of things inside the warehouse. They would've exploded almost in unison. That brought down the rest of the ceiling, including the steel joist that shattered his pelvis."

Garrick's eyes hadn't left the schematic as he pictured the hell unfolding within. All the time, Malik was probably conscious, witnessing every moment. "So the arsonist knew what they were doing."

Jack made a doubtful noise. "Not in this instance. The warehouse was fitted with several fire sensors designed to activate when they detect a heat bloom, as opposed to smoke. They then trigger the sprinkler system and automatically alert the fire brigade. All of that system was still in place. To be honest, somebody with a working knowledge could have disabled the system quite easily. But because the sensors worked, I was able to narrow the radius of error."

A smaller orange circle suddenly sat on top of the yellow one, but this time its centre was positioned on the other side of the victim's body. Six green dots appeared on the plan, arranged in two neat rows. Jack tapped one of them.

"These are the sensors, and this one triggered first. Which suggests it was closer to the heat bloom. You've read the coroner's initial report? The victim was doused with an accelerant. The intention was obviously immolation. I conclude that the victim was struck just enough to render them motionless and then doused. A trail of flammable material was laid for about two metres. A safe enough distance so the killer wouldn't get burnt."

He circled the mouse pointer between the fire exit and the position of the victim. The arsonist's position was between the two.

"I reckon he was planning to make his escape back through the fire exit. What he didn't consider was this shelving unit."

He pointed at a long rack that led from the victim to the middle of the warehouse before an aisle broke its path. Another set of shelves continued to the far wall.

"According to the warehouse plans, these shelves contained turpentine stored in plastic bottles. The victim was probably leaning against the rack when he caught fire. The heat would have easily melted the plastic, discharging the turpentine. The nearest bottles would have poured straight over his head and ignited."

Garrick glanced at Fanta. Her confident flirtation had dissolved to horrified repulsion. The image of the Malik's remains looked as if they were covered in plastic wasn't so far from the truth.

"That would have had two consequences. The melting containers wouldn't have exploded. They would fuel the fire, the flames fanning across the shelving to other items next to them. In this case, the cans that shot through the roof. The second consequence was that a river of liquid turpentine would have flowed across the floor, cutting off the arsonist's escape. He was then forced to run to the front door and raise the shutter, just a couple of feet, so he could crawl under. It's a small gap, but would have provided another large intake of air, further fuelling the conflagration."

Garrick sat back in his chair as he absorbed the information.

"So the murder was intentional, but the destruction of the property, not so much?"

Jack nodded. "My feeling is that the victim would have died wherever they were caught. However, just that this may not be intentional arson doesn't mean the killer isn't inclined that way."

Garrick frowned. "What do you mean?"

"I told you this fire was intriguing. Not because of those specifics, but because it rang a bell. Another incident two months ago. This time in a pub that had closed in Dover. A bloke was killed. Again beaten and covered by an accelerant."

He frowned as he recalled the details. "Your lot was looking into it. I don't think any arrests had been made."

Garrick swapped a look with Fanta. If the cases were connected, then this probably wasn't a simple case of revenge.

Here we go again, he thought.

8

"I must say how impressed I am with these results," Doctor Rajasekar said, peering at Garrick from the side of her computer monitor. "Aside from your blood pressure, which is not good. I'm increasing your dosage. Just five milligrams, so we can see what effect that has on things."

Garrick was buoyed by the positive assessment. He had been dreading his scheduled visit to his doctor and pointed out that was probably why his blood pressure was so high.

Rajasekar took off her thick framed black glasses as she spoke. "I'm taking you off the sleeping tablets. Were you still taking them?"

Garrick shook his head. "I'm falling asleep quickly enough, but I do feel jaded most times. No matter what I do."

"Have you thought of a holiday? A relaxing one on a beach, or in the countryside. Nature is a good healer."

"It's tempting."

Doctor Rajasekar folded her arms on the desk as she framed the next question. "And how are we otherwise?"

"You mean, am I still mental?"

"Mental health is a critical component to anybody's well-being. With all you have been through..."

"I won't lie. I think about bad things most mornings and just before I fall asleep, but I'm no longer anxious about it."

"Talking things through with a–"

"No!" Garrick snapped firmly. "No psychologists. No professional listeners."

"Feels of paranoia, disappointment, depression – they're not uncommon for even the most–"

"I'm dealing with things on my own terms!"

He could see that she was poised to argue, but thought better of it. She gave a small sigh of defeat and put her glasses back on.

"And the hallucinations?"

The words hung heavy in the air. It was another sign of just how much Garrick had changed. In the past, he would have put up a relaxed, joking façade. Now he was more of a mind to nip such questions in the bud.

"Nothing. A slight headache every now and again."

"Headache or migraine?"

"Migraine." The doctor nodded and made a note on his computer file. "But I can deal with it," he quickly added. "It's not debilitating."

"Good." Again the smile returned to her face, which made Garrick wonder if it was purely a cosmetic one that she gave to reassure her patients. "I don't think we have to see one another every fortnight. Shall we make them monthly? Unless you feel things are slipping back..."

"Monthly is fine." He'd rather it be never again, but that wouldn't happen for a long time.

.   .   .

He LEFT the doctor's office feeling unusually angry. Walking straight out into a rainy grey day in Tunbridge Wells merely added to his mood. He zipped his Barbour jacket closed and turned the collars up to protect his neck. He was irritated that the damn thing didn't even have a hood. It was a gift from Wendy, but what use was it if he was going to get wet?

Garrick checked his temper. It had been a thoughtful gift to replace the one that had been stained with blood. He took a breath and headed up Church Road towards his parked car. He'd parked close to the BBC studios where Molly Meyers worked. The young reporter had catapulted to media fame after trailing Garrick's now-famous art case. She had also been the victim of torture and kidnapping at the hands of John Howard's disciples in order to punish Garrick. He was worried about bumping into her, as they hadn't spoken since he visited her in the hospital shortly after the ordeal. He'd seen her on TV a few times during his convalescence, but he'd made a point of not paying too much attention.

The rain increased from a shower to a downpour. Garrick angled his head down as it stung his eyes. Water splashed around his feet, and the heavy rain created a mist of fine particles smothering the flagstones. A few cars and vans passed, but many more were parked closely together up the hill, some so tightly that the gaps between them were so narrow that a pedestrian couldn't cross over, which is what he needed to do. Glancing for a chance to cross was when he saw the figure on the opposite side of the street power walking up the hill. Its long black coat was bent as the person mirrored Garrick and leaned into the storm.

Garrick increased his pace, now looking ahead for a break to cross the street. There was something about the way the figure was keeping pace with him that he didn't like, so he slowed down.

As did the figure.

Paranoia, Rajasekar had warned. Was he really being paranoid, or simply overly suggestive regarding her idle comment?

When he looked up again, he caught a flash of movement as the figure's head quickly moved to look straight ahead. He'd caught the tail-end of a glance in his direction.

Galvanised, Garrick quickened his pace and this time he didn't take his eyes off the figure – a difficult job as parked traffic on both sides kept blocking his line of sight. Then he got lucky - a gap between two vans parked back-to-back. It was just enough for him to squeeze through, but his shoulders smeared the raindrops on their rear windows. Then he was out in the street and jogging diagonally up the hill, towards the busy main road junction.

He was so focused on tracking the figure that he didn't see a private hire taxi take the corner at speed. He heard the horn sound and felt the rush of air as the vehicle swerved around him, but made little an effort to slow. With his heart pounding in his chest, Garrick hopped onto the pavement and spun around to watch the taxi power down the hill.

Then his head snapped around, expecting to see the figure behind him.

There was nobody there.

He wiped the rain from his eyes, fat drops dripping from his eyebrows. There was no sign of the figure, and no place he could have crossed over. Garrick took a few steps back down the hill, glancing into the parked vehicles, just in case. The figure could have easily entered one of the buildings –

although he thought they would have been moving with considerable haste.

His heart hammered away worse than before. He tried to think why seeing the figure had made him so anxious. It was on the opposite side of the road, so not technically following him. And who would follow him, anyway?

He recalled the whole kidnapping case still had loose threads, including a woman who had posed as a technician and planted spyware on the computers of two victims. Although DCI Kane thought she was just an unwitting techie for hire, used by the perpetrators, she had never been identified.

The familiar bustle of the busy street, with shoppers hunched under umbrellas and buses splashing through overflowing gutters, helped ease his angst.

"You're being ridiculous..." he muttered.

He glanced at his watch and realised he'd be late for his next meeting, but that didn't stop him from lingering outside the window of a card shop, the window filled with cute stuffed bears of every colour. He debated buying one for Wendy as a furry sign of support that she should quit her job if she was unhappy. When was somebody too old to receive a teddy bear? Would that make him look completely out of touch?

Feeling anxious, conflicted, and old, he hurried to his parked car.

JACK WEAVER DIDN'T SEEM annoyed that Garrick was twenty minutes late. The rain had cleared on the hour and a half drive to Dover, and the Fire Investigation officer was waiting outside the remains of the gutted Red Dragon pub. His orange hi-viz coat, emblazoned with 'Fire Investigation Officer' on the back, was open to cool him down, and he sucked on a vape which left him wreathed in mango scented smoke.

"Bad habit," he said, switching the e-cigarette off, "but safer than its alternative."

"Sorry to keep you waiting."

"No problem. You'll need this." He tossed a yellow hard hat to Garrick, who fumbled and dropped it. "The structure is relatively safe, but the high winds recently may have knocked something loose. Better safe than sorry in this game."

The site was surrounded by an eight-foot-tall plywood fence, with a padlocked door matching the pub's own entrance. Jack fished a bunch of keys that were attached to his belt by a chain. It took him three attempts to find the right one to open the padlock. The hinges were stiff as he pushed it open and gestured for Garrick to enter.

Jacked pulled the wooden door closed behind them with one hand, while holding a bulky flashlight in the other to light up the dingy interior. Despite the months that had passed, the stench of burning was still heavy in the air. With a constant melody, water dripped from many points across the ceiling, forming dark, infinite pools that hid treacherous obstacles.

Jack used the flashlight as a pointer as he ran it across the bar. "The victim was Tim Selman. He was found lying on top of the bar, just there." He took out his mobile and unlocked it with facial recognition. He had the report up. "Petrol was spread across the bar and furnishings. We found the remains of the plastic jerry can tossed in the corner. It was melted almost beyond identification, so contained no forensic evidence. The fuel was ignited and spread very quickly. The victim was still alive as the flames spread. Unable to escape."

"Was there any video evidence?"

"Nothing on any traffic cameras. We're not too far from the port, so the area is well covered."

Garrick circled around the remains of the bar, which was little more than a few stumps. The shelving had kept its basic shape, but all details had been scorched away.

"The fire rapidly spread down here. This time the smoke alarm had been disabled, so it quickly spread upstairs."

"There was nobody living here?"

"Just the guy who died. His family had left him months earlier. He was the owner. The pub was losing money hand-over-fist, but he was still carrying out building work. An extension to the back. It could have easily been seen as a suicide or insurance claim."

"I'm not seeing the similarities between cases. Other than the obvious."

"The thing that made me think it was similar is that the victim still had their wallet on them. Valuables upstairs were left untouched. There was even still money in the till behind the bar."

"It wasn't a robbery. It was cold-blooded murder."

"I always thought of it as an execution."

Garrick ran his fingers over the wall. They came away covered in black soot. If Jack Weaver was correct, then was there something connecting the two murders, or were they random attacks perpetrated by a psychopath?

The smell was turning Garrick's stomach, and he didn't wish to spend any more time here than he had to, but he was glad he'd seen the crime scene with his own eyes. It made more of an impression than flat incident photographs. Outside, he looked at the partially built, and now heavily fire damaged extension, as he emailed his team asking them to look for connections between the two cases. There was a message from Drury, who wanted to see him before the end of the day, and a missed call from Wendy, who – as usual – hadn't left a message.

They were walking back to their cars when Weaver's radio suddenly went off in a flurry of urgent chatter.

9

I f there was one thing that Garrick missed about regular police work, it was the power of the old blues 'n' twos. The ability to cut a swathe through traffic with just a flashing blue light that had motorists parting like the Red Sea, terrified they'd been pulled over for speeding. It was second only to driving a marked police car at 65 in a 70 zone and betting on who was brave enough to overtake.

Jack Weaver's battered red Fire Investigation Vauxhall van pelted down the A2 at almost 80 mph as he responded to a terrace house blaze in Faversham. Two engines had been deployed to a house fire. As it had been an unusually calm three days for the fire department, Jack hadn't seen the harm in turning up early, and since it was in the direction Garrick was taking back to the station, he thought he'd tag along for a change of pace.

They arrived to find the fire crews had quelled the worst of the fire. Thick black plumes of smoke rose from the windows and the portion of roof that had collapsed. It was a small, terraced house, and fortunately the fire had been contained in the one building, but the smoke damage had inched across the walls of the neighbouring homes.

Two ambulances and a police car sat further back from the bright red, curtain sided Volvo FL8 fire engines – or appliances, as Jack kept calling them. The vehicles' curtain sides were drawn up, thick hoses snaking between parked cars towards the house. The occupants of the house: a middle-aged woman, a teenage girl, and a pre-teen girl, were being treated for smoke inhalation in the back of the ambulance, but otherwise had avoided serious injury.

Garrick kept back with Jack, speaking to the uniformed policewoman charged with keeping a crowd of gawping neighbours back, several of whom recorded the action on their phones.

"A neighbour saw the smoke and called 999," she said. "She banged on the door, but there was no response. Another neighbour kicked the door down and found them unconscious and the fire out of control in the kitchen."

"Carbon monoxide from faulty gas appliances is the most common cause," Jack said. He indicated to the ambulance. "So they had an extremely lucky escape."

Garrick was impressed with the calm, coordinated movements of the fire team. It was not a job he had ever fancied doing, and the extreme perils they regularly faced turned his stomach. Even with the flames almost extinguished, he could feel waves of heat pulsing from the building, chasing away the chill breeze.

With his skin prickling, he had a rush of unwelcome thoughts of the agony the two arson victims must have endured in their final moments. He heard the mother's muffled sobbing from behind an oxygen mask and caught the words *"pan fire"*.

Jack raised an eyebrow. "The most mundane things can have the biggest impact on lives."

"That's why I always prefer to eat out," Garrick said. "Also, I'm a terrible cook."

THE INCIDENT ROOM was empty when he returned to Maidstone Police Station. Fanta had left thirty minutes earlier, and Harry had spent the afternoon collecting information on Danny Summers, Phyllis Carlisle's son-in-law, as well as chasing statements from people who knew Sajan Malik. He could see his young DC had made the most of her time as the file on HOLMES was up to date, and the evidence board had been populated with both arson incidents.

He hung his Barbour coat on the back of his chair, spent several minutes making a matcha green tea in the communal kitchen area, giving brief *hellos* to the various officers passing through that he recognised, then returned to his desk and read through the report Fanta had assembled on Tim Selman, the owner and victim of the Red Dragon. He had run the pub for four years. During this time, its reputation soured with increasing incidents of assaults inside and out, and business inevitably dropped off. He'd spent a lot of cash trying to give it a facelift and a more family vibe, including the new extension. That hadn't worked, and Selman tumbled into debt. It appeared that he'd also borrowed the money from the wrong person.

Predictably, the DC investigating his murder had trouble getting information on the Russian loan shark, but Fanta had diligently called her and got a more nuanced story. The word on the street was that the Russian had laid pressure on Selman to repay the loan, but nothing too drastic as Selman was paying him *something* back. The DC suspected the Russian had ties to other small criminal operations, so wasn't too keen on drawing official attention to other areas of his business. Further poking around had revealed that the Russian was surprised by Selman's murder and had battened down the hatches, suspecting that it was done by a business rival trying to bring him down. Unfortunately, that's where the investigation ran out of steam.

Fanta had written a set of notes as she tried to connect the deaths of Tim Selman and Sajan Malik. The two men had little in common. Malik had been unemployed for three years since losing his job as a mechanic in Leicester. Residents in the block of flats where he lived considered him a quiet man who kept himself to himself. His attacks on helpless victims may have been driven by desperation. Prior to that, he had no criminal record, nor any affiliation with Dover.

Selman was Kent born and bred, although he had lived in Essex for a period of time. He'd had several jobs before taking on the role of pub landlord, including working as a porter at a hotel in Colchester, where he had been fired – and subsequently arrested – for planting spy cameras in the women's toilets. He'd also served six months prison time for aggravated assault two years later.

Garrick stared at the mugshots of both men, next to photos of the destroyed buildings. Jack Weaver felt the incidents were connected, but Garrick wondered if that was nothing more than wishful thinking on the inspector's behalf. It could just as easily be a coincidence, and Garrick knew the dangers of running an investigation down a blind alley.

It was several moments before he realised Drury had entered the room and was regarding him with a frown. How long had she been there? He sprung to his feet, feeling the unfamiliar touch of embarrassment. He couldn't remember the last time he'd been embarrassed. It must have been back when he was a spotty teenager in Liverpool.

"Sorry, ma'am. I was lost in thought."

"So I see."

She entered and closed the door behind her.

"Normally, when I ask my staff to see me, I expect they come to *my* office."

"Shit... um, sorry. I..." he had completely forgotten about their meeting.

Drury gave a thin smile and waved his concern away with one hand. Garrick wasn't used to such displays of camaraderie from her. It didn't bode well.

"It's OK. Your office is larger than the broom cupboard they give me here." She crossed to the evidence board and cast her eyes over it. "Do we have another psychopath lighting up our streets?"

"Not sure about that yet."

"We live in interesting times," she said, almost under her breath.

"I'm not entirely sure that's a good thing, ma'am. There's a lot to be said about boredom."

Drury sat on the edge of the desk and pushed her thick, black glasses up the bridge of her nose in a thoughtful gesture. She had put on weight since her gardening leave, but it suited her. After everything she had been through, he couldn't see a blemish in her confidence. Garrick thought that if she ran for Prime Minister, she'd win in a landslide. However, there was a marked different to her demeanour. An uncertainty he'd only seen once before when she had taken him into her office and told him about his sister's death.

"DC Wilkes will be joining you tomorrow."

"Oh, that's good news. He's missed."

"Mmm." There was a note of disapproval. "And what are you going to do about this relationship between him and DC Liu?"

Garrick hoped the surprise didn't register on his face. While his team knew about their romantic entanglement, he had hoped it would have stayed away from senior channels.

He shrugged diplomatically. "Absolutely nothing, ma'am. I've got two of the finest DCs in Kent, and they've given their all to every case. After Fanta's injury, Sean never faltered." Even though everybody blamed me for what had happened, he added silently.

Drury stared but didn't to push the issue.

Garrick realised he was still standing rather too formally, so sat back down. "And what about Chib? Any word?"

"Do you want her back?" The question contained a layer of ice. She had been forced to plant DS Chibarameze Okon as per DCI Kane's orders. After recent events, Drury had made no secret of her not wanting the woman back.

"I need a DS."

"You now have such a reputation that you'll have a queue of volunteers for that role."

Garrick felt uncomfortable. Molly Meyers had thrown him into the public spotlight, and since then he'd been recognised by complete strangers while out in the restaurant or walking down the high street. He was inherently a private man, and that made him uncomfortable. But it wasn't as bad as the whispers he heard of admiration from the lower ranks. He was more than aware of the animosity that caused by his peers. He'd disliked enough fellow officers for the very same thing. Rumours build and reputations are tarnished by good deeds.

"Let's face it, Chib knows all about me." Literally. She had known about his health problems, his personal relationship with his sister, John Howard, and even Wendy. All as part of her job. All he had known about her was that she came from London and was engaged. Now he knew far more important details – she'd risked her life to save his on more than one occasion; she had integrity; and she was well-liked by the rest of the team.

Was. After the true nature of her role had been exposed, the trust levels had dramatically dipped. Despite all of that, she had still requested to rejoin them.

"You know that I wear my views on my sleeve," Drury said. Garrick nodded; subtlety wasn't her strong point. "I'd hate to have her back. But if you want her…"

"She fits in here."

Drury huffed. "Your team's becoming a collection of oddballs."

"No, ma'am. It always has been one. It's just that you're only noticing now." Garrick couldn't stop a mischievous smile, which only served to deepen Drury's scowl.

"OK! Fine!" She wagged a finger. "But I'm telling you, she is bad news, David. I'm not questioning her abilities, just her loyalty."

He could see his decision angered her, so he folded his hands over his stomach and said nothing.

Drury gave a sniff of disappointment, then waved her hand dismissively. "What does it matter what I think? I may not be around to witness her stabbing you in the back. Again."

"Why not?"

Drury's lips tightened. "When you get close to a Commissioner who turns out, not so much to be bent, but to be a homicidal maniac, people begin questioning your competence."

Garrick swelled with anger. "That's stupid! Nobody else saw what he was!"

"Except you. You caught the snake in the den. Killed him." She didn't seem too upset about that detail. The man had died right in front of Garrick, and he still had the occasional nightmare about it. "So I should be basking in your reflected glory." She sighed. "Turns out that glow around you is radioactive. There needs to be public sacrifice, and those higher up than me think it should be me."

"They're sacking you?"

"Oh, nothing so crass. They'll reassign me. Much better for the department's optics. Nothing's been decided, of course. But the warning signs are there."

"Maybe I could speak to somebody..."

That got a smile from Drury. "Oh, David. Sweet, but stupid. Firstly, they won't listen. Secondly, you don't want them to think we're in cahoots. You still have a career, and if the powers that be got wind of that... they'd put you out of harm's way, too." She reacted to the surprise on his face. "This goes all the way up to White Hall. To the Prime Minister. The Home Secretary is being bombarded to make sure nothing like that ever happens again. Haven't you been watching the news?"

"I don't bother when I'm not on it."

Drury gave a snappy laugh. "On top of which, we're facing budget cutbacks. Not freezes, actual cutbacks. They're looking to trim wherever they can." She circled a finger around the room. "I wouldn't expect your team to swell in size just yet." Her mood suddenly darkened. "It's important to make sure none of them upset the apple cart. Even you, David."

Garrick knew he would get nothing more out of her. Her vague warning just fuelled his paranoia. A warning was one thing, but what was it she couldn't tell him?

10

Rambling had been an activity that Garrick didn't see any point in. He prided himself on spending more time strenuously avoiding it than participating, and he felt healthier for it. But fate had its own opinions on what he could or could not do, and early in their dating regime, Wendy had suggested it a dozen times, each of which Garrick – or work - had conjured up an excuse to pass. Then his luck ran out during his convalescence. Pointing out that he now needed to exercise, Wendy had ushered him into activity. Weekends would never be the same, and he now found himself on his third scramble through the countryside.

"It's just a terrible system," said Duncan Cook for the umpteenth time since they had gathered at the carpark in the High Elms Country Park near Orpington. His nasal whining tone had rubbed Garrick up the wrong way when they'd met on the first walk, although he was far too polite to even hint at it. When Duncan had latched on to the fact that he was a policeman, that had somehow bonded him closer, as if having a lawman on his side would validate Duncan's constant nit-picking. "I mean, how is stopping in the middle of the carriageway possibly safer?" He issued a stuttering laugh that made Garrick increase his pace.

He had been lectured on Duncan's hatred of the smart motorway system, which had seen the removal of the much-trusted hard shoulder across most of the UK's motorway network. In the old days, motorists in trouble could pull over to the emergency hard shoulder on the left and wait for assistance. That option had been removed to add an extra lane and increase traffic flow, but Duncan insisted its removal had increased danger, as the stricken vehicle was now left stranded in the middle of the carriageway while signs warned other motorists of the hazard. Garrick hated that he agreed with Duncan, and had made the mistake of acknowledging so at the beginning of the conversation. He tried to tune him out as he looked ahead. Wendy was near the front of the eight-strong pack, animatedly talking to her friend Judith, and giving the occasional look behind and smirking when she saw Garrick's discomfort. The two club organisers, Mike and Stu, led several yards ahead, while behind him came a middle-aged red head called Sonia, who seldom spoke, smiled, or made eye contact, but was apparently a regular attendee and kept the club's blog up to date. Larry brought up the rear. A bear of a man with a subtle hint of Jamaican ancestry who belted out songs as he trailed behind and occasionally cajoled Sonia. On the surface, Garrick looked like the nadir of health compared to Larry, but the huge man never stopped, never complained, and always completed the trails no more than a dozen yards behind everybody else. It was an easy walk to Downes, where Charles Darwin's house was open for visitors, tucked behind Biggin Hill Airfield. The plan was to have a pub meal there. An hour to walk there, another back, Wendy had insisted it would make for a pleasant afternoon.

Fifteen minutes in, and Garrick was hating every second of it. He suspected it was some sort of punishment Wendy was inflicting because the last few nights he'd been back from work late twice, not really because of his caseload, but because of the lack of progress. Jack Weaver had sent a few emails trying to link the two cases, but still they found nothing concrete. DC Lord had spoken with Rachel Summers, Danny's wife, who confirmed her husband had been home on the nights in question. He wasn't expecting much from the case, but to have it fizzle and die over a lack of evidence was depressing for any detective, and that wasn't improving his mood.

"I can't see it going back to the way it was," Garrick said, already panting for breath. He immediately regretted resuming their conversation as Duncan launched into a tirade of aggressive agreement.

They exited the park and ambled down a narrow country road. The sun came out from behind spectral white clouds and warmed Garrick's face, lifting his mood. He soon found himself walking next to Sonia. He was so desperate to abandon Duncan's incessant stream that he flashed a smile.

"Have you walked this trail before?"

Her eyes widened in alarm when she realised that he was addressing her. Garrick prompted her with another smile.

"Er... y-yes," she stuttered, her eyes darting everywhere rather than at him. "Why?"

"I haven't had time to check the club's blog, and I believe you write about the walks and put pictures up..."

"Email any pictures to the site," she said so quietly Garrick had to strain to hear.

"I'm not taking any," he assured her. "I like to see things with my own eyes, not through my mobile."

She nodded in grave agreement and fixed her eyes on the road. Garrick glanced at Duncan, who seemed to be revving up another barrage of complaints, so he rapidly sought to push Sonia.

"What line of work are you in, outside of this?" he gestured to the surrounding trees.

"You're a policeman."

Garrick tried to ignore how she had avoided the question. It was a detective's lot in life to pick up on all the social *faux pas* people inadvertently made.

"A detective." He didn't know why he said that, but at some level he thought it was somehow less intrusive than a uniformed copper.

"I saw you on TV." Her lips tightened. Garrick couldn't work out if she was star-struck or terrified. "Several times."

"I wouldn't believe everything you see on the telly. I was probably babbling rubbish of some sort." That got a flicker of a smile. He indicated to Wendy, who was now much further ahead. "Wendy said you're new to the group. Well, apart from me."

"Duncan, then me, then you. We're the newbies. But it's been almost a year. Something to do at the weekend," she said by way of explanation.

The conversation didn't blossom, especially when Duncan joined in. Garrick was exhausted and in an abject state of misery when they reached the small village of Downe and sat for lunch in The Queen's Head. Garrick and Wendy ordered a ploughman's and a cider. The alcohol was a rarity for Garrick, and it tasted divine.

"Enjoying being out?" Wendy asked during a break in the

raucous laughter that had been encircling the table. Mike and Stu were the life and soul of the gathering and brought out everybody's better nature. To Garrick's surprise, he was enjoying himself.

"Aside from the walking, it's not too bad."

"Good. Mike was saying that several groups were banding together for a charity walk at the end of the month. A twenty-four-hour hike for heart attack research."

"Bloody hell, twenty-four hours'd give anybody a heart attack!"

She playfully hit him on the arm with the back of her hand. "There are breaks in the walk for power naps and food. Shall we do it?"

Garrick couldn't think of a worse torture. He nodded. "Why not?"

Wendy beamed with delight and a hint of relief. "That's great. I told him we would. And you could really get a lot of sponsorship from the station."

Garrick quietly groaned. He hadn't done a sponsored-anything since he'd been in school. He was always the kid who suffered the teacher's withering look when he came back with a couple of names scrawled in pencil – just his family, of course - raising the princely sum of two quid. Before he could change his mind, Wendy turned her back on him and was telling everybody they'd both be taking part.

Garrick checked his phone as the conversation turned to the route and strategy needed to complete such an endurance marathon. With no pressing need to be in, there was nobody in the office and nothing to report. He got the feeling that budget cuts were already kicking in. There was an email from Jack Weaver. A single line: *I think I may have something!*

It was sent an hour ago. Garrick replied: *what?* He hesitated from sending it, as it felt too curt. He wasn't much of a texter and had grown up writing emails with as much floridity as a formal Victorian letter. He pressed send and put the phone down face up so he could see the response.

As lunch ended, Wendy ordered another cider, and the group took the collective decision to visit Down House, where Charles Darwin had lived. As they left the pub, Garrick checked the phone. There was no reply from Jack. Whatever it was, it would have to wait until Monday. When they reached the house, Garrick completely forgot about the message. He'd always had an admiration for Darwin and was hooked. He caught Wendy's knowing smile and wondered if she hadn't planned to soften him up with this all along; a form of loving blackmail for making him perform a hellish charity walk.

THE WEEKEND WAS MIGRAINE-FREE, and Sunday was spent sitting on the couch with Wendy, surfing between television shows. It was only broken by her taking an hour-long video call with her mother, during which Garrick started reading a biography of Darwin that Wendy had treated him to in the giftshop.

For most people, it would rank as an average or boring weekend. Garrick smiled softly and enjoying the most relaxing time he'd had in recent memory. Every doubt about hastily moving in together was expunged. As they lay in bed, he found the exhaustion of the previous day's ramble drawing him to sleep. Half-asleep, he encouraged Wendy to quit her job.

You only have one life, he told her. *It's your duty to live it.*

. . .

CLUTCHING a sponsorship form for the charity hike, Garrick felt like he was in school again as he pinned it to the notice-board in the police station's communal refectory. Then he entered the Incident Room, and the mood shifted to one of a high school reunion. Harry Lord and Fanta Liu were already in, and a smiling DC Sean Wilkes was arranging his desk.

"Sir, nice to see you back," he said, standing.

"I was going to say exactly the same thing." He looked around the room. "And I believe Chib will be joining us." He caught the look between Lord and Wilkes, but ignored it. "I asked for her, just in case you were wondering. You all know she's bloody good at her job. So good that she had us all duped." He made sure he met everybody's gaze. Nobody looked away; and nobody looked pleased with the news. "But we were all fighting on the same side, just from different angles."

From their silence, he regretted mentioning it and spoiling Sean's return.

"We'll get some doughnuts in for lunch to celebrate us all being back in the furnace." He indicated the evidence wall. "In the meantime we have a case. A murder in an industrial estate. It may be connected to another incident in a Dover pub. Which isn't our case, but the DC there has run out of steam." He rubbed his hands together. "So, has anybody seen the light over the weekend?"

Attention focused on the evidence wall, but no opinions were forthcoming.

"There's every chance they're not connected," said Fanta eventually. "It's not like fires are uncommon. I mean, compared to shootings, stabbings—"

"Point noted. The fire investigator thought they may be." He suddenly remembered Jack Weaver's cryptic email. He hadn't checked his messages since Sunday morning and there still wasn't anything from the fire investigator. Garrick suspected that it couldn't have been too important and was forming the impression that Jack was a man who wasn't thrilled by his job and was seeking escape. Or was he projecting Wendy's circumstances on him?

Harry suddenly spoke up. "I tell you what, that Rachel Summers is something else." His smile faltered as all eyes turned on him and he realised how inappropriate that sounded. "I mean, the way she looks." He caught Fanta subtly shaking her head to stop him. "I mean, her body." He was tripping over his words. "More bloody muscles than I have!" he snapped. "She's a bodybuilder." To clarify, he mimed lifting weights.

Everybody burst into laughter, enjoying his discomfort.

"Christ, Harry. I thought I'd have to give you a warning there," Garrick teased.

"You all bloody knew what I meant." Harry glowered. He was never happy to be the butt of the joke.

"Sounds like she and Danny are a perfect match."

Fanta crossed to the board and tapped the picture of Tim Selman. "Me and Harry tried to find any connection with the Summers and him. Nothing. We don't think they're the right suspects for his death, and he and Malik aren't connected." She suddenly clicked her fingers as something occurred to her. "Unless it's their name! Sajan. Selman. Both esses!"

Sean sniggered quietly.

Garrick sighed. "Remember once when I said there were no bad ideas? That time has passed."

"What about the alphabet killer in the States?" she said defiantly.

Sean corrected her. "That was the Zodiac Killer, Fan." He

was rewarded with a scowl.

"No, she's right," said Harry. "Three kids in the States. All had the same letter in their Christian and surnames."

"1973," said Fanta smugly. Her comment was aimed squarely at Sean. "And their bodies were dumped in towns beginning with the same letter as their names. It's unsolved. As I recall, one of the suspects was a firefighter."

Harry shook his head. "You can always count on the Americans to be bizarre." He caught Garrick's expression and instantly regretted speaking. "Sorry, sir. I'll get the brews going." He quickly left the room before Garrick could recover.

The phone on Harry's desk rang, and Fanta shot over to it so she couldn't be pulled further into the conversational quagmire. Garrick felt his cheeks flush. He knew Harry had meant nothing by it, and the weekend was the first time that he hadn't thought about his sister. Now the inadvertent references had brought it all back, and he wondered why he had heard nothing from the Flora Police Department in Illinois, who was originally handling the case. Since a car had been found with his sister's DNA, and that of another victim, across the state line in New York, it had widened into a Federal investigation and came under the auspices of the FBI. That was probably why he had heard nothing. But with the connection to John Howard, it also meant that DCI Kane would know more about what was going on. He should call him.

Fanta put the phone down and spun in her chair to face Garrick.

"That was the hunky Jack Weaver," she said with a deliberate needle in Sean's direction. "He thinks he's found a connection between the cases. A witness."

11

Against his better judgement, Garrick allowed Fanta to tag along when he agreed to meet Jack Weaver. With no pressing leads to tie the team up, and conscious that an idle unit would draw the attention of those seeking budget cuts, he sent DC Wilkes out to interview some more of Malik's known associates that Harry had uncovered.

They didn't have far to travel to the Fire and Rescue Training Centre, where a group of six volunteers were wrestling a hose, gushing water at a fraction of full power towards a blazing tower. Even with two of them directing the hose, they were doing a terrible job of getting the water anywhere near the target. That made them laugh, which in further spoilt their aim. Jack and another instructor watched on in amusement.

"I hope they're never going to be out in an emergency," Garrick said, shaking his head.

Jack grinned. "Don't worry. Volunteers visit people to give advice, check smoke alarms, that sort of thing." He lowered his voice. "We don't need them underfoot during an emergency."

They spent a few more minutes watching the volunteers switch roles – and then succumb to pratfalls as they lost control of the hose. Jack took them to the commissary and treated them to dark coffee. The smell was bitter enough to prevent Garrick from even sipping it. He was a tea man, and since moving in with Wendy, had been the subject of her experimentation in serving increasingly exotic blends. After more idle chatter, the conversation turned to Jack's discovery.

"Sorry for the radio silence over the weekend. I suddenly thought you might be switched off and enjoying family time."

"I was rambling." Garrick saw both Jack and Fanta looked puzzled. "Hiking. Not talking aimlessly, although I've been accused of that, too."

Jack put his phone on the table as if to show them something, but didn't turn it on. "Arsonists tend to enjoy returning to the scene of the crime to witness the destruction. They get a kick out of it. Crews try to photograph any gawking crowds that turn up at a fire to see if there are any familiar faces."

"You've found one?" Fanta said in surprise.

Jack hesitated and tapped his phone. "Sort of." He activated his phone and played a video clip taken on the night of the warehouse fire. "This is body cam footage from one of the fire fighters attending the scene."

The footage was shaky and uneven as the autofocus struggled to switch between the dark industrial park, then the sudden bright flames of the warehouse fire lit up the area. It was the first time Garrick had seen just how bad the blaze had been. Flames licked forty feet into the air with audible roars. The fire crew's voices were muffled as they shouted commands. At one point, the cameraman turned and headed back to the fire engine to check the water pressure. Even though it was in the dead of night, a crowd of spectators had formed behind the appliance. The blue emergency strobes flashed over them, providing the only illumination other than the flames.

Jack glanced between the screen and the detectives. Then he tapped the screen to pause the footage, then used his finger to scrub the timeline back a few seconds.

"Her." He indicated a woman at the front of the crowd. The image was dark and out of focus, but her Asian features were clear enough as she watched the fire with an incredulous expression.

Garrick's shoulders bobbed. "So what? There are four other people there with the same gormless look."

Jack held up his palm as a defence. "I've seen her before. I know this sounds bad, but I have a thing for Asian chicks..." he mumbled. Garrick could hear Fanta's cheeks flush. "And I've been looking through footage of other incidents, but so far have drawn a blank."

Garrick turned the phone for a better look at the woman. "Let me get this right. All you have to go on is a vague recollection of seeing this woman somewhere before."

Jack nodded. "In connection to an incident. Look, we're not living in Japan. This is Kent." Jack didn't appear to realise that he was bordering on racism. "My folks brought me up old school, so I apologise for not being woke." His smile dropped under Fanta's stern look. "I mean nothing by it, and surely that's irrelevant if we can save some more lives?"

"All you're going on is a hunch?" said Garrick.

"Aren't hunches the things that solve cases in police movies?"

Garrick hated that he was correct. In his experience,

hunches were like truffle pigs; one of the best skill sets to undercover the facts.

"I appreciate this isn't the hard lead you were hoping for." Jack's confidence was reasserting itself. "But in my line of work, we must put a lot of faith in our assumptions. Often, that's the best way of seeing the whole picture."

"WHAT A WANKER!" Fanta exclaimed as they crossed the car park.

"You've quickly changed your tone. Are you going to put that in your report?"

"*Chicks?* What a neanderthal!"

"It takes all kinds," Garrick pointed out as they reached her car.

"That doesn't make it right."

Garrick was trying to be sympathetic, but had noticed several emails on his phone, including the picture of the woman that Jack Weaver suggested they identify.

"Run the image through facial recognition and see what comes up. Worse case, we can at least dismiss her and Jack's hunches," he said.

"Me? I'm not running his dating service!" She caught Garrick's darkening look and huffed in defeat. "Okay." She opened the driver's door. "Back to the station, then?"

Garrick was reading an email that had caught his attention.

"Sean found out that Danny Summers' van was caught by a bus lane camera in Chatham the night Malik was killed."

"When he was allegedly home? Which means his wife is covering for him," she added thoughtfully. "But what's in Chatham?"

Garrick was already scrolling through Google Maps. Chatham was a fifteen-minute drive from the warehouse fire in Snodland that took Malik's life. He pinched the phone screen, zooming out so that he could see all of Kent.

"I'll tell you what's in Chatham. The A2. The quickest way back to Ramsgate if you're trying to avoid the M2 and M40."

"Like if you're speeding away from the scene of a crime, for example?"

Garrick couldn't hold back a smile. "Is that a hunch, DC Liu?" His grin broadened as he watched Fanta struggle to hold back an expletive.

"Yes," she finally admitted. "But based on the excellent nugget DC Wilkes found."

Garrick opened the car door. "Nugget? I don't know about that. He may just have cracked the case."

A twitch of annoyance pulled the corner of Fanta's mouth. Garrick was pleased to see that professional rivalry was alive and well within his team, no matter what Drury thought.

BACK AT THE STATION, the incident room was alive with more activity than just two men should be able to make. Sean and Harry had delved into examining Danny Summers' with gusto. Fanta ran the blurry photograph through a photo recognition system that checked against criminal records and social media. Her request was held in a virtual queue as other units were busy demanding time on the system. Another symptom of cutbacks. Forensic lab work was getting increasingly delayed, even in the most serious cases.

She set about logging their visit into HOLMES. Jack Weaver's laddish attitude still angered her, so her choice of words was less than tactful. She wondered how much trouble she'd be in for calling him a twat in an official document.

Towards the end of the day, Garrick and Fanta were listening to the fruits of their labour. Sean spoke as he placed Danny's picture in the centre of the evidence board.

"Despite his hard man image, Summers has lived nowhere else but Kent. He's a bit of a mummy's boy and has no criminal record. I was hoping to speak to his mother, but thought it may trigger too many alarm bells. She was bound to warn her son that I was nosing around."

Garrick nodded his approval.

"He's a courier for DCL TACTICS, so I spoke to his manager without mentioning Danny directly."

"Any complaints?"

"On the contrary. He's one of the best drivers they have. He's even had compliments from customers for going the extra mile."

Garrick was surprised. Customers, and he counted himself in that group, were always the first to complain when things went wrong, but very few ever acknowledged decent service.

Wilkes continued. "He handles local deliveries, and from what I could gather, he's been *everywhere*: Snodland, Dover, Chatham – just tick the boxes."

"Told you he had prime suspect written all over him," Harry said.

"I've been to all of those places," said Fanta. "And I bet both of you have, too."

Sean held up a finger as he continued. "Interesting fact. When he was twelve, his family home was damaged by a fire. It was started when some fireworks stored in a cupboard went off. He denied it, despite being an only child..."

"Flimsy." Fanta crossed her arms.

A ghostly smile crossed Sean's face. Whatever game of one-upmanship was occurring had bypassed Harry completely. He was affronted by DC Liu's dismissal and stood to approach the evidence wall.

"Hold on a minute. It was Rachel Summers' mum that Malik attacked. Now, it seems Danny is a mummy's boy, and it's Rachel who wears the trousers in their relationship." He put a picture of Rachel up at the side of the board. "She works security at Westwood Cross Shopping Centre in Ramsgate and has one hell a reputation. Heavy-handed is the diplomatic way of saying it."

"So your theory is...?"

"The wife pistol-whips hubby in getting revenge."

Garrick pulled a face. "From what you've said, he doesn't seem the killer type."

Harry was getting excited about his theory. "Ah! That's if we assume he was intending to kill Malik. If the intention was to hurt and maim... and then it got out of hand..."

Fanta scoffed. "Out of hand? By burning down half an industrial estate?"

Garrick leaned thoughtfully back in his seat.

"The fire report indicated the arsonist left by the front door, not the side, which would have been more secretive. Jack Weaver thought it was because the fire got out of control almost instantly."

Fanta pointed a finger at Harry. "You're buying his idea, sir?"

"You have to admit, it's the best lead we have."

"It's the only lead!" Fanta exclaimed.

"Exactly. Good work the both of you." Sean and Harry beamed like Cheshire cats. "He was lying about being home, so let's have a chat with him in the morning."

12

"I did it!" Wendy exclaimed as Garrick entered the house. He was mid-yawn as she threw her arms around him and kissed him on his stubbly cheek. "Ouch. You need a little grooming there."

"Did what?" The front door had barely shut, and he was already feeling in a daze.

"I handed in my notice." Wendy danced on the spot, stiffly swinging her arms back and forth while twisting her waist. It was a move Garrick vaguely recalled the kids calling *the floss*. "I quit! I quit!" she sang.

"Wow! That's... that's great." Garrick was struggling to find the words. "How do you feel?" She looked at him side-long, mid-dance. "I mean, obviously, you're delighted. Which is terrific."

She stopped the jig and was suddenly worried. "Are you sure about this?"

Garrick forced a big smile. "Absolutely!" He crushed her with a hug. "Best decision you've made. Apart from deciding to give me a second chance after our disastrous first date."

That first encounter often haunted him. He still didn't know what she saw in him to even consider a second date. She called it fate; he called it a moment of insanity.

It wasn't the only thing haunting him that night. The adrenaline Wendy had felt from making such a big decision was wearing off, and midway through their dinner – courtesy of the microwave and Tesco's range of Finest ready meals – they both hit a wall and agreed on an early night. They would celebrate tomorrow.

But the moment the bedroom light went off, Garrick tossed and turned. Thoughts of a deep slumber vanquished into the darkness, and his mind prickled with thoughts about his sister's death.

He jolted so severely that he was afraid he'd wake Wendy. He'd been drifting through a series of micro-sleeps. A quick glance at the clock on his phone showed that it was now 1:14 am. He'd been dreaming about his sister peering down at him as he'd been wheeled into the operating theatre. His subconscious had seized the image and was regularly using it to punish him. Or was he punishing himself? He accepted that his original vision was an episode brought upon by stress and the anaesthetic, but that didn't make it feel any less real, and it had woken him on more than one occasion.

But not now.

He sensed something else had jolted him awake.

The silence became filled with the blood pounding in his ears. The street outside was hardly a busy one, especially at night, but somehow it seemed as if that too was holding its breath... waiting for something...

Downstairs... was that a noise?

Garrick slowly climbed from the bed. Wearing an old pair of running shorts and a faded T-shirt with the caption

Straight to VHS! picked out in crumbling letters, he hardly looked like a threat. He crept to the door, aided by a sliver of light through the curtains coming from the streetlights outside. After pre-operation events, he'd hinted that Wendy should have something innocuous lying around for security, such as a baseball bat, but she hadn't acted on it.

He reached the door – and stubbed his toe on the corner of the chest of drawers. A stab of unproportionate pain shot up his leg, and he grit his teeth so as to not to call out aloud. Trying to ignore the throbbing toes, he stepped out onto the landing. Stopped. And listened.

It came again. The faintest of sounds that put him in mind of something light dragging across the bare floor, made by somebody desperate to keep silent. Garrick's heart pounded as he took the first few steps down the stairs. He could handle himself, but not against an armed intruder. The sensible solution was not to creep around in the dark, but to make as much noise as possible; but he'd never been the sensible one.

The floorboards squealed as they took his weight. Any advantage he had was now shattered. Fuelled by a rush of anger, Garrick thundered down the remaining steps, hoping it was enough to surprise a thief. His hand snaked out and fumbled to find the hall light switch. He'd always thought the moment a home became a home was when locating the light switches in utter darkness was nothing more than a reflex action. The fact he couldn't find one now was worrying.

After knocking two coats off their pegs, his fingers found the switch, and he turned the light on. Nothing looked amiss. The front door was securely shut and latched with a chain. He hurried into the living room, lighting it up. Everything was as it should be, including his laptop under the table.

Only when entering the kitchen, and flicking the lights on, did he see that the backdoor was ajar by an inch. He dashed to the sink and picked up a knife from the draining board. A pointless act as the kitchen was empty. Nothing had been disturbed here. He dashed to the backdoor and peered out into the garden. It was too dark to see anything, but it was also so small and concreted over that there was nowhere to hide.

Then he remembered that he'd been out earlier to take the wheelie bin around the front for collection the next morning. He mustn't have shut the door firmly. The wind was blowing, causing the chain hanging from the kitchen blinds to sway over the countertop, creating the noise he'd heard.

With a trembling hand, Garrick gently closed the door and locked it. He quietly returned to bed, feeling more awake than he had all day. Wendy was on her side, making occasional snoring noises. She'd slept through the whole thing.

THE LACK of sleep was affecting Garrick more than he cared to admit. He'd been irritable from the moment his alarm had gone off, and things had spiralled downwards from there.

"You lied. It isn't a question, it's a fact."

Danny Summers sat on the sofa with his arms folded. Garrick and Harry had called at the house at 8 am, with the sole aim of catching him before he left for work. Rachel had already left for the gym, then straight to work, and Phyllis had been up preparing breakfast for herself. Danny had given monosyllabic answers until he pointed out that they'd now made him late for his shift. Garrick had zero sympathy for him.

"If you'd told the truth, we wouldn't be here."

"I wasn't thinking straight, was I?" Danny leaned forward. "You mentioned Malik had been assaulted, but you didn't make it clear which night we were talking about. Simple mistake."

Harry moved behind Garrick like a predatory shark. While Garrick needed the perception of having some muscle as backup, he had to admit Harry's constant circling was irritating him. He was having trouble recalling exactly what details he had divulged about Malik.

"Sajan Malik was murdered that night."

Danny unfolded his arms and propped his elbows on his knees. A quick glance in Phyllis's direction, and he couldn't hold back a small smile. "What a shame," he said with absolutely no sincerity.

"What were you doing in Chatham that night?"

"Driving home."

"At two in the morning?"

"I was on a late shift and off work the next day and had accidentally taken a set of keys home." Danny shrugged as if that answered everything.

"You work for DCL TACTICS. Out on a delivery, were you?"

"Down the depot."

"In Chatham?"

"Aylesford. It's not a secret."

Garrick felt a jolt and for a moment was worried he'd experienced a micro-sleep. No, it was a surge of something clicking into place.

"Aylesford is right next to Snodland. That's where Malik was killed."

Danny slumped back in his seat and shrugged. "And how

was I supposed to know that? That's where I was on my way out until you made me late."

Garrick didn't trust coincidences. He loathed them, yet they were a trick the universe played on the unsuspecting. They were not the rarities people assumed; they happened with alarming regularity and made police work far more complicated than it needed to be. Now he had motive and a location that put Danny a mile from the murder scene. But it still wasn't enough to tip the threshold of evidence, that ambiguous scale that needed to tilt in order to get a conviction.

And now Danny Summers' guard was up, Garrick felt it would be even more difficult to reveal the truth.

"Who did you pass the keys to? I need a name."

Danny lifted his hands in a small, helpless gesture. "I didn't stop to see anybody. I just popped in and hooked them on the board."

"So nobody saw you."

"I didn't see anybody." He shrugged again.

Garrick glanced around the living room, hoping for some divine inspiration. The furniture and ornaments were dated. The money had been spent on the television and sofa, suggesting that was where the family spent most of their time. There was only one picture of him and Rachel on the wall, taken in a sunny pub garden. Wearing shades, they were raising their pints to the camera. He glanced at Phyllis, who was still quietly listening.

"Mrs Summers dropped you off at the bingo." She nodded. "And she later picked you up?" Another tilt of the head. "What time?"

Phyliss hesitated. "I'm not sure. Just before midnight, I suppose."

Sajan Malik's murder happened about an hour and a half later. Plenty of time to drive there, Garrick thought, so it wasn't the best alibi to offer. Criminals usually took a lot of time constructing intricate and well-timed cover stories to mask their crimes. The basic principle of an alibi was that it covered the exact period the crime was being committed. The more elaborate the alibi, the easier it was to poke holes and tear the thing apart. The most common bullshit warning was when a suspect claimed they were doing something at *exactly* the time the crime was being committed. Even if that information hadn't been given to them. Danny Summers' excuse was troubling because it covered both ends of the spectrum.

"Why not take the motorway and get home quicker?" Garrick asked.

"I spend most of my time on motorways. I'd drank a ton of coffee so was feeling wired and knew I wouldn't sleep when I got home." Another shrug.

"But not wired enough to realise you were driving through a bus lane?"

Danny didn't comment. Garrick was struck by a whim. He showed Danny the picture of the woman Jack Weaver suspected.

"Does she look familiar?"

Danny leaned closer, and his eyes narrowed as he examined it. "Haven't got my reading glasses..." he muttered, then shook his head. "Nope. Who is she?"

Garrick put his phone away and considered what to do next. He was convinced that Danny Summers was lying, but lacked any concrete evidence. He was equally sure that the enthusiastic Fire Inspector was barking up the wrong tree. He glanced at DC Lord, who returned a subtle nod of support. Harry had obviously come to the same conclusion.

Garrick sighed. "Mr Summers, I'm detaining you on suspicion of murder—"

Danny slumped back in his chair. "What the hell?"

Harry was already on his phone to notify the rest of the team. Garrick continued reading Danny his rights and hoped the forensic team would find the smoking gun.

THE DETENTION MEANT that the rest of Garrick's day was bound to paperwork, interviews, and more paperwork. They had to wait for several uniformed officers to arrive before they could search the house, while two officers escorted Summers to the Maidstone station to check him in.

Throughout this, Phyllis Carlisle didn't raise any protest and remained quiet, only speaking to confirm her daughter's workplace. Summers' white transit van was parked on the street outside, the same one that had been caught on the camera. It was a battered white model with patches of rust hanging it together and displaying all the same care and attention as their house. There was a small, paved garden area at the back, with an old fridge dumped in the corner and a wooden shed that wasn't padlocked and contained tins of paint, thinner, and a Raleigh racer with two flat tyres.

It was after lunch before Summers had been processed and assigned a solicitor, who was dressed in jeans and a trendy top and looked as if he'd been dragged out of a Club 18-30 to attend. Garrick and Lord sat with them in the station's interview room and waited as the DVD recording device whirled a pair of discs up to speed. A bleep from the system notified everybody it was recording, and Garrick read out the usual statements before delving into the questions. As expected, Danny Summers issued a string of "no comments" that made the entire time an exercise in futility. It was all an annoying part of the game. Garrick didn't have any solid evidence, and Danny knew that. It could well be that there was no evidence to be had, but again, that was all part of piecing things together.

With nothing more to be said, the interview was over after ten minutes and Summers lingered in a cell until he was released under investigation. Garrick called the forensic team to speed their inspection of the van along. At least he would jump the queue now this was a murder investigation, but it would still take some time. Which meant the team was back to twiddling their fingers as they awaited a break.

That happened much sooner than he expected when he answered a video call from DC Fanta Liu.

13

The camerawork was appalling, but despite Garrick's pleas, DC Fanta Liu was far too excited to hold her hand steady. She and DC Sean Wilkes had gone to the Westwood Cross Shopping Centre in Ramsgate to speak with Rachel Summers. Rachel was on duty and took a fifteen-minute break so they could talk outside.

At six-foot one, she towered over the detective constables. The sleeves on her security uniform were rolled to the elbows, revealing an intricate web of tattoos, and showed off biceps larger than Sean's. More tattoos teased the edge of her neck, and Sean had speculated how much of her body was inked.

She stuck to her story about taxiing her mother to the bingo in the transit van, and when pressed about Danny's sudden dash back to work, she merely nodded and claimed she'd been asleep, but he'd told her about it the following morning. She was consistent and unfazed when told her husband had been taken in for questioning. And, like Danny, she gave no hint of remorse at learning that Malik had been killed, but stopped short of showing any signs of pleasure.

The interview had been another tick box exercise for the investigation that nobody had thought would bear fruit. Wilkes thanked Rachel Summers for her time, and they parted. They were ready to head back to the car when Fanta remembered she needed tampons and headed to Boots. The mere concept of a woman's bodily function flustered the otherwise cool Sean Wilkes, and he agreed to wait for her in the car.

Purchase complete, Fanta hurried from the pharmacy and almost ran into a cleaning woman mopping a milkshake from the floor. Her heart skipped a beat when she recognised the woman from Jack Weaver's photograph. There was a Costa across the way, with tables outside and a line of sight to the cleaner. Fanta dashed to take a seat, ignoring the disgusted snort from a pair of women who were already zeroing in to claim the table. From there she video-called Garrick.

"It's definitely her," Fanta insisted.

Garrick felt as if he was tiptoeing through a minefield of political incorrectness. "It was a terrible photo. We can't be entirely sure." The image search had come through an hour ago and had drawn a blank. The odds that Fanta had bumped into the woman in the middle of a shopping centre were astronomical. As far as Garrick was concerned, they had stumbled beyond the realms of coincidence and into the Twilight Zone.

"I'm sure of it," Fanta insisted. "The camera on my phone isn't the best, and she's probably too far away, but I walked into her. I'm certain it's the same woman."

Garrick knew better than to argue with his young DC. "Okay, see what you can find out."

THE NEXT DAY, Garrick drove to the DCL TACTICS hub in Aylesbury. It was another bland warehouse amongst a grey industrial complex. During the drive, Jack Weaver had called him to ask if they had any leads on identifying 'his' suspect. Rather than get his hopes up, Garrick gave a vague "we're still working on it," and turned the conversation to what he'd found at Summers' house. The paint materials in the shed were purchased in any hardware shop and not the ideal weapon of choice that a dedicated arsonist would employ. Garrick hoped that some of Sajan Malik's DNA evidence would show up in the van, but forensics was still processing the contents. Weaver insisted that Garrick keep him posted, leaving him with the belief that the fire inspector did indeed fancy himself as a police detective.

Patricia Royston was a senior shift manager of the DCL TACTICS hub and welcomed Garrick into her office. She was in her late thirties, but looked far too young for such a senior position. She wore her hair in a smart bob and had an ingrained pleasant smile. Garrick had to be careful about casting dispersion about Summers' character. If the man was innocent, the accusations could still stain.

"I didn't hear about any missing keys," she said. "But to be honest, it happens. We're in the middle of expanding and upgrading all our systems. I don't know if you saw the huge extension being built at the back? It's going to be all touchless technology, so no more misplaced keys."

Garrick sipped the water he'd been offered. He was still feeling exhausted from another sleepless night. His anxiety over his sister's death was increasing, but he didn't know why. He'd decided to keep quiet and not tell Wendy. If it got worse, he may have to consider asking his doctor to put him back on the sleeping pills. He suspected their absence was causing the side effects.

"It's just so we can rule him out of our investigation." He indicated the stack of files on her desk. "You know how it is with needless paperwork."

Patricia smiled in agreement. "That I do." She typed a message on her desktop computer as she spoke. "Well, if he came back, then he'd need to swipe his ID to gain access. We'll have an in-and-out log. I'll ask security to get that for you now."

"What's Danny like to work with?"

"Excellent. I wish we had more like him. Between you and me there is a junior managerial slot opening up I think he would be perfect for." She pulled a face. "But that would mean losing him from the driving pool, which would be a shame. He's been here a while, but only full-time in the last month or so."

"So, no problems with him, then?"

She looked levelly at him. "No. Customers love him." She looked back at her screen as the messenger app gave a low bing. "Ah, here we go. He swiped in at 1:32 and out again at 1:34."

Garrick made a note of the times. They tallied with Summers' own account, but still placed him a mile from the crime scene as it was happening. The news hadn't moved his investigation needle any further.

With Royston praising Danny, there were no further questions Garrick could think of, so he thanked her and left.

As he was in the area, Garrick decided to visit the crime

scene. The warehouse entrances had been sealed with large plywood sheets that were synonymous with abandonment. The two warehouses either side were open for business, but the black smoke stains hadn't been touched, and would no doubt remain there for a long while, as the owners put through their insurance claims.

The car park in front of the warehouses still showed signs of the fire, with the tarmac in front bubbled and melted slightly, and there were signs of emergency vehicles rushing to a halt as they attended the incident. They'd left behind skid marks, not caused by the rubber on their tyres as was the common misconception, but from the tyres heating the surface and essentially melting it. The marks couldn't be washed away, which is what made them ideal for crash investigators, but they would slowly wear away with the passage of traffic.

Garrick walked through the industrial estate's gates, which remained open for twenty-four-hour access, and stepped onto the pavement of the busy dual carriageway. On the other side, a cold-grey steel fence ran parallel to the road, segregating the industrial estate from the houses beyond where Malik lived. Using the pedestrian crossing, Garrick made it to the narrow pavement on the other side of the road. He considered Sajan Malik's path from his house, in the dead of night, through a gap in the railings, which he found a hundred yards down the road and into the industrial estate.

It suddenly occurred to him that none of the team had visited Malik's home. Uniform had attended and found it locked up. What had driven him outside?

Garrick slipped through the gap in the railings and found himself on a strip of land filled with trees and overgrown brambles. Rusty beer cans, fast food wrappers, and other detritus were caught in the plants. He slipped down a short incline to the road below. Malik would have had to scramble up there on all-fours. The homes immediately across from the fence were two-storey apartments, built by the developers to entice commuters. Some had garage ports to the side, and they couldn't be more than a decade old. He followed the curving road, designed with occasional cobbled chicanes to slow traffic flow. Townhouses lined either side of the street, creating a concrete canyon that echoed every scuff of Garrick's shoes on the pavement.

Two hundred yards later, he was at another set of two-storey apartments. Malik had lived on the ground floor. Garrick inspected the blue front door. There was no visible sign of forced entry. He made a call to schedule one of his team and a forensic officer to wipe the apartment down in the hope they would find any DNA traces from Danny Summers.

Garrick glanced around. There were over a dozen windows that had a view of the apartment. If anybody had been kicking the door down or arguing on the step, then they would've been overheard. As it was, no witnesses had come forward. That suggested Malik knew his attacker.

That threw another spanner in his working theory. As far as he knew, there had been no direct contact between Danny Summers and Sajan Malik, and even if there had been, why would he open the door to the son-in-law of the woman he attacked? It made little sense.

Garrick returned to the Incident room with conflicting feelings. It was empty, his team strewn across the county picking at the pieces of a case that he was increasingly suspecting may not get solved. He noticed that somebody had pushed the Tim Selman incident to the side, as their connecting threads remained a mystery, if there were indeed any at all.

It was two days later before Garrick had any more movement on the case. Fanta and Wilkes had been in and out of the office, but Garrick had left them to their own devices and had only seen them once. Harry Lord had finally gained entry to Malik's apartment, and a forensic team had swooped through.

Harry noticed a pair of muddy trainers had been left at the front door, with a pair of battered shoes and another set of Adidas, with a hole in the sole, tossed into a closet under the stairs. Of course, he didn't know how much footwear Malik possessed, but wondered if he hadn't left the apartment in such a hurry that he was barefoot. A call to the coroner failed to offer answers. The collapsing ceiling had crushed Malik's pelvis, and his legs had been blown off in an explosion. Whether he was alive or dead, naked, or wearing ski pants, the coroner couldn't say. It was yet another unanswerable question, and Garrick was already tiring from the vagaries an arson case created. He was even in danger of respecting Weaver's skill sets and thought he'd been too judgemental on the man's keenness. Optimism was most definitely an asset in fire investigation.

Further news came in regarding the forensic sweep of Danny's Summer's van. There was no DNA evidence that indicated Sajan Malik had been in it.

The day somehow dragged itself out for Garrick, with only Harry for company. He ambled through the commissary and was shocked to see that his sponsor sheet was filled with names. So many that another two sheets had been added. A quick tally showed that his infamy across the department had already raised £330 in pledges. He'd secretly been hoping that nobody would sign up so that he could back out of the hike, but there was no hope of that now.

He returned to the incident room to be greeted by a Fanta and Sean, who both wore expressions of extreme smugness. Garrick didn't even say hello as he knew he was in for a lecture. He dropped into his chair, linked his hands together, and looked expectantly at the pair.

"We've cracked it," Fanta said proudly. Wilkes was about to correct her, but she steamrollered over him. "Well, we will."

She moved the photo of the Asian woman Weaver had sent them to the top middle of the evidence wall. "Amanda Chin. British with Malayan parents. She lives in a caravan park in Whitstable."

If she was expecting a round of applause from Garrick, then she was greatly mistaken. He shucked his shoulders, prompting her to continue.

"She works with Rachel Summers in the shopping centre. They know each other."

"Know, or...?" Harry left the sentence hanging.

"Well, they're colleagues. She's a cleaner. Rachel is on security. They've been seen talking dozens of times. It's not beyond anybody's imagination that the subject of her mother's attack was brought up."

Garrick could already see where Fanta's imagination was taking her, and he injected his voice with a dose of enthusiasm.

"So you think that Rachel Summers hired her to work as a hitwoman and exact her revenge?"

Her hesitation spoke volumes.

"Maybe in a bizarre cleaning accident?" Harry added with a chuckle.

Sean took a slow step backward, leaving his girlfriend in the firing line. That, more than the heckling, pissed Fanta off.

"So you think it was a coincidence she was caught on camera at the fire at two o'clock in the morning, miles from her home?"

That wiped the smile from Garrick and Harry's faces. Seizing the opportunity to wind Fanta up had clouded some of the facts.

"A good point," Garrick conceded. "But sketchy reasoning."

"Then why else was she there?"

"Friends?" Sean said. "Maybe she knew Malik." She gave Fanta an apologetic smile. "I did say the hitwoman thing was a stretch."

Fanta ignored him.

"Or she got a lift from a friend..." Garrick mused. "We can connect her with Rachel Summers, but not with Danny."

"If they work together, the probability increases that the three of them could've met."

Fanta clicked her fingers as she tried to recall something. "What's that film?" She offered no other clues but continued snapping her fingers, demanding an answer.

"Star Wars?" Garrick couldn't help himself.

"Harry Potter?" laughed Harry. "The Muppets?" he added with increasing hysteria.

"The double murder one. With the fat guy..." Then it came to her. "Throw Momma from the Train." Nobody was any the clearer. "Billy Crystal and Danny DeVito. They meet and decide to commit one another's murders as an alibi."

"Are you sure you don't mean Strangers on a Train?" Garrick hazarded.

"Whatever. But the principle..."

Garrick puffed his cheeks as he considered. "It's no better or worse than what we had. If it really is the same woman."

Fanta bridled. "Why not ask the fireman? He's the one with the hots for her."

Garrick was already considering an unofficial surveillance sojourn, but hesitated. Such ventures never seemed to have happy endings for his team, and he couldn't do with another overly dramatic incident. Fanta had a point about Fireman Jack. He'd be the best person to verify if it was the same woman. He ended the briefing by congratulating Liu and Wilkes, although he wasn't sure what about, and called Jack Weaver.

"You're sure it's the same woman?" Jack asked. "Because living in a caravan park seems a bit... well, not what I expected."

"I'm surprised you had any expectations. And that's why I think it would be handy for you to come along and double check."

"I won't be able to make it until after eight."

"That's fine."

It would be dark, and they ran the risk that Amanda Chin would stay in for the night. In that case, Garrick could flash his badge and do a couple of routine enquiry calls to flush her out. He hung up and remembered that he and Wendy had agreed to have a little celebration over quitting her job. Now he was unlikely to be home before eleven at best. He was sure she'd understand, but it reminded him that living with a partner – while wonderful – came with plenty of restrictions he didn't have before.

As he was leaving the office, Fanta intercepted him.

"Before you go, Guv," her formality swayed the Richter scale of how pissed off she felt with being belittled, "I thought you should know something else I've just found out about Chin. I ran a list of her previous addresses. She used to live in Dover. Around the corner from the Red Dragon, in fact." She treated him to a thin smile.

14

Paradise Cove in Whitstable was a sprawling caravan park on the edge of town, a mere hundred-yard stroll to the beach. With seventy static caravans, most boasted their own shower rooms, kitchenettes, and double bedrooms. It was a home away from home for tourists and was advertised as a step up from 'glamping'. Twenty-three of the caravans had permanent residents, although their leases stated that occupants could only stay there ten months of the year.

Amanda Chin had been renting a caravan fifty-six for the last two months. Rent was paid in advance, which included water, security, and access to a laundry room. Heating came from the butane tanks that also powered the gas stoves and were the responsibility of the resident.

Garrick parked his rattling Land Rover in the car park. On the way here, it had developed a symphony of new sound effects that heralded its impending death knell. With him having to support Wendy for a little while, there was no room in his finances to buy a new car. He lamented that John

Howard had gifted him a brand-new Range Rover in a twisted act of psychological manipulation. It was a fine machine that was now locked away in an evidence pound somewhere and would ultimately be sold at auction once Howard's case had been closed. Garrick had never even sat on the luxury soft-leather seats.

It had been dark for a while, and the clear skies scattered a frost across the neatly mowed grass and rooftops. It sparkled when it caught the security lights lining the narrow paths that formed a web across the park. The whole effect added a pleasantly exotic air, a nice departure from the crowded, soulless housing estates cast across the country. All designed with the same bland ethic, so it became almost impossible to discern one part of the country from another.

Garrick caught his rampaging monologue and stopped it. He sounded like Duncan Cook. The older he got, the more things he found to complain about. He hated that he was aging so stereotypically. Shivering from the cold, he considered that his life hadn't turned out quite the way he imagined.

As if to irritate him, his migraine was making an unwelcome return.

The lights were on in Amanda Chin's caravan, and he could see the occasional movement inside. Walking past, he caught the low sounds of a television and guessed that she was home for the night. He may have to resort to Plan B and knock on the pretence that he was conducting a routine safety check. That wouldn't be worthwhile if Jack wasn't able to confirm her identity.

Fanta's latest bit of intel had reluctantly convinced him she was onto something, although he still found her Strangers on a Train theory ridiculous. His padded Barbour jacket failed to keep the evening chill out, and he shivered hard. His phone slipped from his numb fingers and fell screen-down on the path.

"Crap..." he mumbled as he stooped to retrieve it. A simple action that had his knees groaning and had him wondering how he was going to survive the twenty-four-hour hike. As he feared, the screen now had an ugly crack curving from the bottom left corner to the top right. "Dammit!"

To make matters worse, there was a text message from Jack telling him he couldn't make it, as he was being held back at work. The trip had been a complete waste of time. He'd sent the text an hour earlier and suggested that Garrick hold off so they could both go tomorrow.

Angry for a wasted night and a damaged mobile, Garrick spun on his heels and marched back towards his car. He decided that Fanta and Jack could make the visit tomorrow. It was the weekend, and he was determined to cut himself off from work and try to enjoy his new relationship.

Three yards later, a distinct gassy smell wafted on the gentle breeze blowing in from the North Sea. He stopped and turned, trying to locate its source. And at that moment, Amanda Chin's caravan exploded.

A furious orange fireball rolled from the front of the mobile home where the butane tank was connected. The powerful explosion tossed the entire caravan up in the air. The shock wave shattered windows of the other homes as it knocked Garrick onto his arse.

As he watched, the caravan flipped a lazy one-hundred-and-eighty degrees, the plastic panelling flapping as flames smothered it. It crashed back to the ground on its roof. The weight of the under chassis tore the weakened walls apart, and the unit collapsed on itself, partially crushing everything inside.

All Garrick could hear was a loud tinnitus ringing; his vision swam; and his migraine screamed at his brain. He slowly noticed the worsening situation around him. Patches of grass had caught fire, and burning debris fluttered down like hellish snow. Residents were now spilling out of their homes to find out what had happened.

Garrick drunkenly swayed to his feet and ran towards the burning wreckage.

"There's somebody inside!" he screamed as loudly as he could, but to himself he sounded muffled, as if his own ears were filled with water... or had the explosion affected his speech? This was exactly the situation he was supposed to be on sick leave to avoid.

The heat from the flames radiated a good six feet, and he was forced to raise his arm as a shield to protect his face. Even through his jacket's thick sleeve, the heat prickled his skin.

A man appeared next to him, wearing nothing more than a dressing gown and clutching a fire extinguisher the wrong way around. Many people kept a small extinguisher in the kitchen for emergencies, but Garrick knew statistically that almost none of them knew how to use it, or that fact they had a shelf life and needed to be replaced. He tugged the red canister from the man's hand and spun the nozzle towards the flames. Holding it steady with one hand, Garrick yanked out the safety clip and squeezed the trigger.

A froth of white foam spewed across the flames in front of him. The extinguisher was designed to tackle electrical fires, but Garrick couldn't afford to be picky. He aimed the stream onto an angled wall panel that suggested something was underneath. He judged it to be a kitchen cupboard and edged closer.

Acrid black smoke blew in his direction, making him cough. Smoke inhalation killed more people than the flames, and in the state he was in, it wouldn't take much. He hunkered down, hoping to avoid the plume, but his eyes stung. He forced them open and used his foot to raise the corner of the smouldering wall. He glimpsed an arm underneath.

"She's here!" he bellowed, then set about layering more foam over the panel.

With only twenty-five seconds of life, the extinguisher spluttered and died with a pathetic trail of white spittle. Garrick tossed it behind him and dropped to his knees. He felt a piece of debris slice into his thigh, but he ignored it and used his shoulder to support the wall. The dressing gown wearer and another man dropped to all-fours and reached for the woman's arm.

"Pull her out!" snapped Garrick as the heat began singeing his right ear and hair. His eyes were so itchy he forced them closed. He could feel the movement as they pulled the woman past him.

"Clear!" somebody yelled.

Garrick dropped the wall and crawled away from the burning wreckage on his hands and knees. Every time his left knee touched the ground, a jolt of pain shot through it. When he judged he was far enough away, he rolled to his side and coughed the smoke from his lungs.

He felt hands on him as somebody tried to help, but he couldn't understand what they were saying. His eyes were fixed on the body of Amanda Chin, illuminated by the dancing fire that cast teasing shadows that hinted of movement and life. If that was possible. Smoke rose from her body. One side of her was scorched black, with chunks of skin glistening with blood.

Garrick couldn't believe that she had survived such a brutal attack.

And an attack it must have been. Coincidences now had no place in Garrick's world. And he had a horrible feeling Fanta may be on to something...

15

His night had been spectacularly derailed. Garrick's assumption he'd be home by eleven turned into 2 am when Wendy picked him up from Canterbury Hospital. He'd been treated for light burns to his right ear, the side of his neck, and the top of his left hand. It was nothing severe, but the skin stung like crazy. He'd been given oxygen to treat light smoke inhalation, but had insisted he was fine.

His attempt at marching out of the private room was hindered by a stabbing pain in his right leg. A piece of metal from the debris had slid into his thigh when he'd knelt. It did some minor muscle damage, and he could see from his trousers when he put them back on that he'd bled heavily. The bottom of the leg was covered in black ash, dried blood, and mud. He looked as if he'd stumbled through the trenches. It also hurt like hell when he walked, forcing him to limp slightly. He and Harry Lord would look like the walking dead when they were next in the station.

The doctors refused to tell him what had happened to Amanda Chin, and it wasn't until a uniformed officer had been sent to check up on him, did he discover she was alive against all the odds. But she was in a terrible state and suffering third-degree burns. He had no doubts that the explosion was premeditated – he was just lost on the *who* and *why*.

The uniformed officer assured Garrick that the crime scene was cordoned off and the fire team and forensic unit were dealing with it. A quick glance at his cracked phone screen showed him that none of his team were rushing to see him. To be fair, they should all be at home, living their own lives until Monday morning. He considered calling everybody into the office for tomorrow morning, or rather, later that morning, as the case had expanded to two murders and an attempted one. Knowing that forensic data would take time, and Amanda Chin was in no state to be interviewed, he decided nothing would change until Monday.

That just left him with the problem of how to get home. His car was still at the caravan park. A taxi would cost a fortune, and he felt cheeky asking the uniformed copper to take him home. The answer revealed itself when he noticed three missed calls from Wendy — all after midnight. Considering it was just after two in the morning, she had shown incredible restraint when he'd told her he'd be back by eleven.

She answered his call with quiet calm, although he could detect her concern when he asked her to pick him up from the hospital. She did so without complaint, and without asking too many questions – especially when her eyes fixed on his bloodied trousers. Garrick didn't need any proof that she was a special lady; but if he did, she'd just confirmed it.

On the drive home, he filled her in about what had happened at Paradise Cove. Even as he described the scent of gas and the ensuing explosion, he marvelled at the fact he could have been standing at Amanda Chin's front door as it exploded. It was doubtful he would've survived. The course of his life had changed in a single split-second decision. Had he looked at his messages earlier, then Jack Weaver might have saved him from all the pain he was in now.

He lapsed into silence as he thought about how the smallest of decisions could change a life. Or end a life. He looked furtively at Wendy. Lit by the dashboard lights it was difficult to see, but he was sure she'd paled. He reached over and gently squeezed her hand, that was gripping the steering wheel.

"Thanks for picking me up."

"Are you kidding? What did you think I'd do?" She forced a smile. "Don't go making a habit of all this, like expecting me to drive you to pick up your car later."

"I'll make it worth your while."

"Oh?"

"Three hundred quid."

"Oh, detective, isn't that illegal?"

"You weren't soliciting, so no, it isn't. That's how much I've raised in sponsorship so far."

Wendy's eyes lit up. "Dave, that's incredible! I've only managed fourteen so far."

"That's lame."

"Although, after seeing your limp, I'm not sure you'll be able to do it."

"It's a couple of weeks away. I'll manage." Garrick was surprised by his conviction. He'd been searching for an excuse to avoid it, and now that he had the perfect one, he felt an overwhelming desire to complete the walk and prove a point. Not to Wendy, not even to himself, but to the universe.

David Garrick was not going down without a fight.

THE THROBBING PAIN in Garrick's leg didn't ease when he woke up the following morning. For a moment, he panicked because he couldn't feel his leg at all. It took several minutes of self-administered massage to bring back a wave of pins and needles. It was just after ten, and he'd slept like a log. For the first time in a while, it had been a dreamless slumber. Checking his phone, he noted three missed calls from Jack Weaver. He didn't have the energy to reply, but knew that he would've heard about the incident at Paradise Cove and wouldn't stop calling until they'd spoke. He resigned himself to do that after breakfast.

He put his phone back on the side table and ran a hand across the crumpled sheets next to him. They were still warm, so Wendy mustn't have been awake for much longer than he was. We a soft smile, he recalled how she had laid him in bed and undressed him – vowing to shred his smoke damaged clothes. Then she lay on top of him, gently kissing his battle worn body and muttering soothing words. Before he'd met Wendy, Garrick's love affairs had been too far apart, and he'd almost forgotten the magical touch a woman could give. The warmth of her body was a complete contrast to the vicious fire he'd experienced earlier and, as tired as he was, he couldn't stop being aroused.

Their clumsy love making probably caused more pain as he shifted position, but the gains far outweighed any discomfort. Entwined together, they were both dripping with sweat, despite the coolness of the room. It was a rare moment of tranquillity, and one in which Wendy started to talk about their future.

With all the bad timing in the world, Garrick struggled to fight the blanket of sleep that was smothering him, aided by her soft, unfocused words.

It was with deep embarrassment that she returned to the room with a breakfast of toast, jam, sliced apple, orange juice and a cafetiere of coffee, arranged on a tray. Garrick shuffled upright in bed as she extended the tray's legs and positioned it over his lap.

"Since when did we become posh?" he said with a grateful smile.

"A hero's healthy breakfast," she said, sitting next to him. "And it's only healthy because we haven't been shopping, so there are no eggs, bacon, or croissants. We'll have to go later."

Garrick tried to ignore the 'we' element, as he spread the remains of the strawberry jam over a slice of toast. While recuperating at home, he'd been unable to avoid the weekly trips to Asda. They were sojourns he never enjoyed and had hoped returning to work would somehow give him a *get out of jail free* card when it came to taking part. He was wrong.

"We can go after you pick up your car," she suggested. "And mum's invited us for lunch tomorrow."

The temptation to return to the office raised its head. Garrick got on well with her parents in the few times they'd met, but he couldn't help thinking that they disapproved of the danger he put their daughter through. Especially as last time, Wendy had to move back in with them because a suspected bomb was parked outside her house. It turned out to be a false alarm. It wasn't a bomb, but a dismembered corpse placed there to taunt Garrick. Apparently, they thought that was just as bad.

"Okay," he said with a mouthful of toast that he hoped would disguise his reluctance for their new weekend plans. He plunged the coffee and poured them both a mug full, using chipped cups he suspected Wendy owned when she was still living with her parents. She thoughtfully buttered her toast until the silence in the room felt unnatural. "I'm sorry about last night, Wend."

"It's fine."

"No, it's not. I said I'd be back by eleven and I, well... things got out of hand."

"You saved a woman's life. If you hadn't had been there, then who knows what would've happened."

"Still..."

Wendy scooped the last of the jam onto her toast. There had barely been enough for the two slices.

"I'll add jam and coffee to the shopping list." She took a small bite and clinked her cup against his. "Cheers."

An uncontrolled laugh spilled from his lips. He had to admire how she was taking everything in her stride. She sipped her coffee and looked thoughtful.

"They're letting me go at half term." She watched him over the rim of her mug.

"That's good." He devoured the toast in two more bites and his stomach wambled demanding more.

"That's in two weeks."

Garrick paused mid-chew. He had no concept of school timetables and had assumed her leaving date would be months away.

"With a week of half-term, two weeks now, they didn't see the sense in having me come back for a last week. It would just confuse the children. So they're recruiting for a new teaching assistant." She sounded disappointed.

"It's what you wanted." Garrick pointed out.

She sighed. "I know. It just feels odd that they can replace me so easily. You're a detective. They don't grow on trees. People like me do."

"There's nobody like you."

She smiled, but wasn't fishing for compliments. "I thought I'd have more time to look for another job, or perhaps do a course and retrain in something new. A university degree, maybe."

Garrick choked on the crumbs of toast trickling down his throat. In his imagination, he'd thought that Wendy would be unemployed for a couple of months as she sought the right job. The thought she'd be at university for a year or two was alien to him.

"Are you OK?" she rubbed his arm affectionately.

Garrick nodded and wiped the tears from his eyes. "Went down the wrong way."

Wendy stared into space. "I thought I'd have more time to sort myself out. I don't even know what I want."

"Who does? I meet people all the time who know exactly what they *don't* want. It's rare to meet people with a rock-solid outlook on life."

"Elon Musk," she blurted. Garrick frowned. "The billionaire space rocket guy. He seems to have his life sorted."

"He's a billionaire. Of course, his life is sorted. We're a couple of quid short of that, so I don't think it's a good comparison."

"How about Alan Sugar?"

Garrick scoffed. "Huh! He's just a lousy millionaire. And a

bit of a dick too, I think. Maybe aim somewhere in between for safety."

Wendy giggled and automatically squeezed his injured leg. Garrick barked out as if he'd been electrocuted.

"Friggin' hell!"

Wendy snatched her hand back. "I'm sorry!"

"It's just my natural reaction when I hear Alan Sugar," he wheezed.

Wendy returned to thoughtful contemplation. "It would be nice to have a brainstorm about it over the weekend."

"Sure. Have a think if there's somewhere we can go for inspiration. London, maybe? We can always have lunch with your parents another time," he added hopefully. She didn't respond. Garrick's work may have dulled his emotional radar, but his empathy was working just fine. He took her hand and gave it a gentle squeeze.

"You'll be just fine. And maybe jumping into this with both feet is a good thing? No time to stall. No time to over-think things. Dive right in and do something that makes you happy. We can cope. For a while," he added, just in case.

She looked lovingly into his eyes. "Where did I find you, David Garrick?"

"On a crappy dating app, after a terrible first date. If you'd waited any longer, then it would have been in a scrapyard, as this old body is getting more beaten up by the minute."

"It makes you look rugged." She traced a finger down the red skin on his ear and neck. It stung, and Garrick sucked in a breath. "Except this. It looks as if you've fallen asleep sunbathing."

"That was the style I was going after."

Out of the corner of his eye, he saw the screen on his

phone light up with another missed call from Jack. There was also a text message from reporter Molly Meyers. He sighed.

"I'd like to get my car back this morning. I've got a feeling there're a few odds and ends I must iron out. Then we can pop out for a big shop."

Wendy nodded. "And while we're at it, maybe we should book a holiday? If you crack this case soon. Prices drop after half term, and it looks as if I'll be free."

She pecked him on the cheek and almost skipped to the bathroom. Garrick was left wondering if she was surfing her train of thought or if he was being emotionally manipulated. Admittedly, there were worse things than a vacation to be blackmailed into.

DURING THE DRIVE to Paradise Cove, Garrick suggested Wendy pop into a few travel agents near their local Asda, hoping she would impulsively decide to do the shopping while she was there. She resolutely didn't pick up on his veiled hint. He kissed her goodbye as she dropped him off outside a line of blue police tape and a uniformed officer who was diverting traffic. Garrick showed his ID card and pointed to his car.

"That's mine." The officer nodded and lifted the tape for him to duck under. Even that feeble movement made his leg twinge. Perhaps he'd been too optimistic in thinking he could still take part in the all-day hike. The thought of missing out now annoyed him.

The remains of the caravan had been cordoned off, and large gazebo covers had been erected to protect it from the elements. It was a clear day, but the wind had picked up, causing the awnings to lean, and lending a chill to the air.

Several yards away, white garden tents had been erected, with several white-clad forensic specialists moving between them. A couple of dark blue police incident vans were parked further behind, next to a red fire investigation unit vehicle.

As Garrick approached, he was surprised to see a smiling black woman approach him.

"Chib!"

"Morning, sir."

Detective Sergeant Chib Okon's smile broadened with the warmth of his greeting. He shook hands a little too formally.

"I'm so happy to see you back. I thought you were due next week?"

"Trust me, I was looking for any excuse to get out of London. Left last night and thought I'd pop into the station to see what I'd missed this morning." She indicated the gutted caravan. "Turns out things have changed little since I was last here. It's back to the usual mayhem and destruction."

They walked to the nearest forensic tent. Chib clocked his limp, but said nothing.

"That's not fair, Chib. Give me credit. I've never blown up a static caravan before."

As they neared, Garrick heard the distinctive Aussie-twang of his favourite techie. He walked in to see the perpetrator in her white forensic onesie, talking to another two junior, similarly clad, techies who were laying fragments of a metal cylinder on a table. She looked up with a lopsided smile as Garrick entered.

"David Bloody Garrick! I figured this shitstorm was yours."

"Hi Zoe. Sounds like you missed me."

"Never a decent murder attempt when you're not around.

You attract them like moths to a bulb." She nodded at Chib. "I see the gang's back together again."

Garrick refrained from answering. He wondered what gossip was circulating the forensic labs about his team. As his last few cases had been high-profile ones, everybody seemed interested in the team's inner workings. He pointed at the gas canister.

"Gas explosion. I could've told you that." He touched his injured ear. "I found some evidence closer to home."

"We're picking up fragments from across the park. Doubtful we'll get all of them."

"I think you'll find one in the hospital from when they yanked it out of me knee."

"Gas canisters don't explode," she said. "They're designed not to. This held butane. Highly flammable, right, but only in contact with a flame. Just that it's inflammable doesn't mean it'll explode when in contact with the air. So even if the case split open, you'd just have a cloud of gas hanging in the air."

Garrick held up a finger to interrupt her. "I'm being a bit dense, but just to check, flammable and inflammable mean the same thing, right?"

"Give that boy an English degree. Quite right. Despite the 'in' part of flammable, it means they'll catch fire very quickly. If you need any further clarification, I suggest you call Stephen Fry and ask. The gas comes out at pressure, so even if you lit a match right at the nozzle, the pressure is too high for the fire to blow back and combust the gas."

"Can we tell if it was in use at the time?"

Zoe gestured towards the caravan. "The fire damage was so intense that I don't think we'll find anything useful from this mess. The fire inspector's out there now. I can tell you what we learn, but beyond that, I'd be surprised we dig up anything useful."

Garrick followed Chib outside and towards the caravan. The smell of burning plastic and wood increased with every step, and he hoped it wouldn't linger on his clean clothing. True to her word, Wendy had tossed yesterday's trousers and shirt into the bin outside, insisting there was little point in cleaning them.

"This is Fire Inspector–" Chib began as Jack Weaver twirled around and looked Garrick up and down.

"Jeez. You got lucky!"

"If I'd bothered reading you email earlier, I would've been even luckier."

Jack turned back to the wreckage. "I think Amanda Chin absorbed all your luck. I hear she's still alive."

"It's touch-and-go," said Chib. "I checked in with the hospital on my way here."

"So what caused it?" Garrick asked.

"Faulty butane cylinder is most likely."

"I was told that doesn't happen."

"You were told wrong. If a valve sticks, you can get blow-back. Even if the flames can't seep inside, butane combusts at one-thousand nine-hundred and seventy degrees. The temperature of a nozzle under a sustained flame could theoretically reach that and – boom!"

Garrick thought back to last night. Wouldn't he have seen a flame near the tank? It was dark and would have shone like a beacon.

"I could smell gas just before the explosion."

"Again, a faulty valve."

"Could it have been deliberate sabotage?" His voice was loaded with meaning.

Jack looked nervously around. "Well, yeah. Of course. The best way to do that would have been to trigger an initial incendiary to break the tank, or at least weaken it. With weakened integrity, the cylinder would have popped."

"I've checked with the site manager." Chib consulted her impeccably handwritten notes that filled a Moleskin notebook. "There is a security camera at the car park entrance, which has been broken for a couple of weeks. It was blown down in a storm. There is a security guard who does the rounds, but in a cost saving exercise, he covers both here and another site five miles away."

"And let me guess, he was at the other site."

"Correct."

Garrick looked around the campsite. It was off season, so the only residents were the semi-permanent ones, and it looked as if all of them had gone to ground. It was as if Chib could read his mind.

"Uniform have already taken statements. Twenty-eight residents were here. Nobody saw anything suspicious. The first they heard was the initial bang."

"And what was Amanda Chin's status in the community?"

"Nobody had anything bad to say. She attended the first two resident meetings, but nothing after that. She's only been a resident for two months. She'd asked a neighbour for help when her satellite dish stopped working, but other than that, she was as quiet as a mouse."

Garrick took the site in. Last night it had a magical aura. A place to step out of the rat race and relax. In the cold light of day, it looked harsh and barren. The last place the lonely or destitute came, like a frontier town. Except this was the frontier to the next life. One that would hopefully offer better opportunities than this one had.

. . .

WHILE GARRICK HAD BEEN PLEASED to see Chib return, it also had made him feel redundant at the crime scene. In one morning, she had efficiently swooped in, assessed the situation, and put all the necessary investigation systems in place. Garrick had nothing to do except deal with a couple of prompts from Wendy to meet in him in Asda.

The glamorous life of a police detective. Even his inner thoughts had turned ironic.

Jack walked with him back to his car.

"There is another option we didn't consider," he said quietly. "That this was caused by Chin herself."

"You mean an accident?"

Jack nodded. "Like those suicide bombers who detonate far too early. What if she was creating an incendiary to use on another target?"

"Have you found any evidence to support that?"

Jack gave a short, gruff laugh. "Give me a chance. I'm assuming the seat of the fire was towards the front, which puts it close to the butane. If it all went wrong, it would have done so in a hurry."

Garrick thought back to last night. The woman had been moving between the front and middle of the caravan. With the bathroom and bedroom at the opposite end, that meant she was active in the middle lounge and the kitchen-cum-dining area at the front.

"Forensics will pick up on anything suspicious." They reached his car, and he stopped to look at the other parked vehicles. One of them was probably Amanda Chin's. Rather than make the painful walk back to Chib, he called her to make sure the vehicle wasn't overlooked, then sent Wendy a message to tell her he was on his way.

"Do you think she'll recover?" Jack said.

"Mmm? Oh, you mean Miss Chin? I hope so. She didn't look great last night. I'll make some inquiries later. Please send me a copy of your report as soon as you're done. Everything counts."

16

David Garrick had never thought he'd be so engrossed and fascinated while walking down the aisle of tinned goods in Asda. He was right. They'd shuffle forwards a few steps, only to have Wendy pick up a tin of potatoes, then compare them with another brand for seconds… or possibly minutes… a process that dragged eternally out. To make matters worse, his mobile phone signal was intermittent and only picked up a couple of bars as he neared the tills and the freedom beyond; a freedom cruelly showcased behind a long glass wall, teasing him about life outside. As they reached the end of the canned goods, his phone picked up a scent of a signal with a text message from Fanta. She'd tried to call him several times; she was at the hospital. Amanda Chin was conscious, but still in a fragile condition.

They reached the chilled section and had been deliberating the ideal pack of sausages when Wendy noticed he was no longer following with the trolley. Instead, he stared at his phone. She sighed loud enough for him to hear.

"What's happened? Has the Bat signal gone up again?"

Garrick looked up. He'd only caught a few confusing words.

"What signal?"

She nodded at his phone. "They can't do anything without you, can they?"

"I am the DCI," he said with an unexpected note of apology.

Did he detect a look of disappointment? Or was it his overactive imagination, because she now smiled weakly and nodded her head.

"At least tell me you'll be back for dinner."

Relieved by the offer to escape, he snatched a pack of fat pork sausages and tossed them into the trolley. His stomach rumbled in anticipation.

"These are perfect!" He rolled the trolley in front of her and kissed her on the cheek.

"Promise!"

He took several steps towards the exit before stopping and turning back. He slipped his debit card from his wallet and pressed it into her hand.

"I'll get this week's big shop. We still have to celebrate you quitting work!"

Then he was away and out of the door before Wendy could remember to ask him for his debit card's PIN.

GARRICK'S LAND Rover had coughed and chugged into the Asda car park, and he dreaded having to ask Wendy for a lift to the hospital. He was relieved when the engine turned over the second time. The gear stubbornly shifted into first, and he crawled from his parking space.

DC Fanta Liu was waiting for him at the hospital reception. He'd called her on the way but got her voicemail, so left a message.

"I thought this was your day off, Liu?" Garrick said, striding across the car park.

"The DS called us all this morning and told us what happened, so Sean and I came in to nudge the investigation along."

"And Harry?"

"His phone's off. I remember him saying something about golf."

Garrick nodded. It was a new hobby Harry had taken up since his injury. Less strain than his beloved five-a-side, but he claimed it was just as much exercise. He'd even tried to coerce Garrick into joining him.

The hospital reception doors automatically swished open as they walked in. Garrick kept a pace behind Fanta, assuming she knew where they were going. Even following her short stride sent a jolt of pain through his injured leg, which in turn sent an involuntary puff of air out of his lips.

"How're you feeling, sir?"

"I've been better. But by all accounts, I could've been far worse."

He'd expected an irreverent quip from her, but she looked pale and just nodded.

"The DS is still at the scene," she said as they reached an elevator, and she impatiently stabbed the up button, "so when we heard Ms Chin was awake, she asked be to come down."

Garrick couldn't help but note that she had avoided mentioning Chib by name and wondered if Fanta was taking DS Okon's undercover role for DCI Kane as a personal insult.

Fanta continued. "She's been awake for just over an hour and is on a lot of drugs. She's suffered fifty-five per cent third-degree burns. A doctor told me fifty per cent is not surviv-able," she said in a quiet voice as the elevator doors opened and they stepped inside.

"Is she able to speak?"

He watched as Fanta seemed to fold into herself. "I'm not sure," she eventually said in a whisper.

Without further conversation, they exited the elevator at the burn centre. Fanta introduced Garrick to Doctor Werner, who was a specialist. Her bobbed hair was tied back in a tiny ponytail so tightly that her face was pinched back, giving her an austere appearance. An appearance further enhanced by the reluctance she projected on Garrick.

"I told your constable here," she tilted her head in Fanta's direction, "That the patient may be conscious, but she's unable to talk."

The patient, thought Garrick. The cool detachment the doctor employed was much the same as his own to help focus on the facts of the matter at hand, a defence against the emotional baggage that came with thinking of the patient – or victim – as a person. With that came complications, entan-glements, and problems.

"I appreciate that, doctor," Garrick said with very little authenticity, "but I need answers only she can give. Other lives may depend on it."

Doctor Werner shifted her weight from one foot to the other as she absorbed Garrick's subtle blackmail. *Help, or else...*

With a weary sigh, betraying countless nights comprising too little sleep, Doctor Werner indicated they should follow and took off down the corridor at a brisk pace.

"She's suffered severe third-degree burns which most people wouldn't survive. Her vitals are fluctuating. She's on fluids, and heavily tranquilised to deal with the pain. Any response she gives you, if most likely an incoherent reaction from the cocktail of drugs in her system." She looked pointedly back at Garrick. "Which makes your endeavour rather pointless, doesn't it?" She led them through a heavy door, into a white corridor that bristled with antiseptic. "The likelihood she'll survive the end of the day is minimal. You'd be making far better use of her time, and yours, by notifying next of kin."

Garrick glanced at Fanta, who still looked reserved. "We may have placed her family in Newcastle, but so far we haven't been able to speak to anybody."

Werner stopped outside a door and gave Garrick a pleading look.

"Are you sure you want to do this?"

"We need to."

With a deep sigh, Werner pushed the door open and led them into a small room. A glass partition segregated Amanda Chin from the rest of the room, with a closed door connecting the two. Amanda lay on a bed that seemed to be little more than a white mattress. A bank of machines monitored her heart, oxygen, and blood pressure, creating a slow electronic backbeat. Three intravenous drips connected to veins in both arms and her inside leg, and a pump steadily wheezed oxygen into her system.

What was most shocking was Amanda herself.

She lay naked, covered in a translucent plastic sheet, through which Garrick could see the hint of dark flesh. The sheet ran to just above her breasts, exposing her neck and head to the air. One side of her face was hard, black, cracked flesh that looked like the aftermath of a barbecue. One ear was missing. In its place, a lump of melted flesh that put Garrick in mind of a congealing candle at the end of its life. Hair had been burned away to the scalp, leaving nothing more than a patch of black and crimson skin. One eye had melted, the lids fusing to her cheek. The opposite side of her face was more recognisable, although not much more. There, her hair was left untouched, and her eyelid swollen so much she'd barely be able to see out.

Garrick felt a wave of revulsion. He understood Fanta's reticence about wanting to see her again. He couldn't imagine the agony the woman must have endured. Was she aware of how disfigured she'd become? If she survived, Amanda faced years of painful reconstructive surgery, yet no matter how intricate the wonders of modern medicine were, she would never look the same. Never be the same. Her life, however long that would be, was irrevocably shattered. Doctor Werner looked at her as if it was something she'd seen every day, which was more or less correct.

"The room is hermetically sealed to avoid infection. Even the slightest bug would kill her in this fragile state." Her hand hovered over a small button. "She can hear you through the intercom. Don't expect much."

Garrick switched positions with the doctor. She stood back near the door. The glowering image of her face reflected in the glass near Garrick's shoulder, like a disapproving conscience. He cleared his throat and pressed the button.

"Miss Chin. Can you hear me?"

If she could, she made no response.

"My name's DCI Garrick. I'm investigating what happened to you." Still no response. He wondered if Fanta would have better luck with her easy charm and ability to effortlessly slip into friendly banter. She was staring at Amanda Chin through the glass, her eyes wide and fearful. It suddenly occurred to Garrick that she may be reliving what happened to her during the house explosion they'd both been involved with. Fanta had been saved by a miracle, but was she now trading places with the patient? Imagining what might have been? He regretted letting her back in the room, then remembered that had been Chib's decision. He was supposed to be back in the bland world of Asda. He pressed the intercom again.

"I'm one of the people who pulled you from the fire. I was coming to speak to you about your job in the Westwood Cross Shopping Centre. About Rachel Summers."

Amanda Chin stirred with the slightest turn of the head and the flicker of fingers rippling under the protective plastic blanket. Her heart rate picked up slightly, as if to confirm she'd heard him.

"Are you friends with Rachel Summers?" There was no additional confirmation, but the ECG sustained its pace and the hand continued moving, fingers working from under the sheet so they could see them gently tapping the bed. Her index and middle finger were fused together. The mass of her hand was raw and black like overcooked sausages – instantly putting Garrick off them for life.

He clocked Werner's look. She was intrigued that he'd got any response. Garrick pressed on.

"Did she ever introduce you to her husband, Dan?"

Again, the fingers trembled, but there was no other acknowledgement. Garrick felt frustrated. This wasn't a coherent response; it was her nervous system firing random signals at the sound of his voice.

"Amanda…" he felt foolish for continuing, but it was as if

Doctor Werner's spirit-like reflection was judging him like some sort of Dickensian ghost. He caught sight of his own reflection. His singed ear and neck were merely dark stains in the glass. "Amanda, did you ever meet Dan Summers?" The ECG continued pulsing; the hand continued shaking. "Did Dan Summers visit you last night in your home?"

With nothing more than spasmodic trembling, Garrick turned to the doctor. "Sorry, but I had to try."

Werner gave the slightest shrug and reached for the door. "She needs to conserve every ounce of strength. Any agitation is detrimental." She was about to open the door when Fanta suddenly spoke up.

"Wait!" She hadn't taken her eyes off the victim, and now moved closer to the glass. "She *is* responding!"

Garrick frowned, but knew better than argue with his junior.

"She has met Dan."

"Fanta, how...?"

She touched the glass, pointing to the hand, which was still moving.

"When you asked if she knew Rachel, it was the same rhythm."

Werner scoffed. "Involuntary motor reaction–"

Fanta cut her off. "And when you asked if Dan had visited her, it changed. Ask her again."

Garrick exchanged a glance with Werner, who couldn't look more disapproving. Before she could object, he pressed the intercom.

"Did Dan visit you last night?"

Now he was looking for it, he saw the change in tempo as Amanda Chin tapped out a response.

"See?" Fanta said excitedly. "It's Morse code. She's saying

'no'." Fanta tapped the glass to mimic. Dash-dot - dash-dash-dash. "Before it was," she tapped again, dash-dot-dash-dash – dash - dot-dot-dot, "yes."

"Holy shit!" Garrick couldn't stop himself.

"Amanda, did somebody visit you last night, before the explosion?"

YES.

"Was it Rachel?"

NO.

The taps were becoming weaker and continued in a pattern Garrick couldn't follow until they faded, and with it her heartbeat sank to the same weak pace it was at before she answered.

"Is she saying who did?"

Fanta shook her head. "It's what she was saying before. I thought I was mistaken, but..." her voice cracked.

Emotional support was an alien concept to Garrick, a man who used to think a consoling slap on the back and a pint later would solve everything. That was before the emotional rollercoaster his sister's death had put him on. Knowing the Force's Human Resources department would have a coronary, he gently put a hand on Fanta's shoulder and gave it a gentle squeeze.

It did the trick, and Fanta sucked in a halting breath. "She was repeating the same thing." She gently tapped the message on the glass. "*Kill me. Kill me...*"

Garrick felt a chill run down his spine.

THE COOL AIR in the car park was a bracing jolt to both their systems, and Garrick reflected that the walk back to the car was always a panacea for whatever horrors they'd witnessed.

Fanta kept glancing at his leg every time he limped. "Isn't that getting any better?"

"After what we've just seen, I hardly think this counts as a war wound."

"If you don't do your sponsored walk, I don't have to still pay, do I?"

Garrick's eyebrows rose in surprise. "You sponsored me? Well, I don't suppose signing the form enters you into a legally binding contract." As usual, there wasn't even a ghost of a smile for his quip. "That was some deduction. How the hell does a Millennial like you know Morse code?"

"Brownies. Then the Guides. I got all the badges."

Garrick wasn't surprised. They reached her car. Fanta toyed thoughtfully with her keys.

"But that's not the question I'm asking. I'm wondering why a cleaning woman from a shopping centre in Ramsgate knows Morse code. Who is she?"

17

G arrick was true to his word on Sunday and didn't immerse himself in work. Chib had taken the reins over the weekend. He'd wanted her back, and she was more than willing to jump into the workload, so he couldn't complain. He told her not to contact him unless it was majorly important. That didn't stop him from stealing glances at his phone throughout the meal with Wendy's parents in Rochester.

Peggy and Brian were pleasant people. She had been a school receptionist, and he had forged a career as a manager for a leading insurance firm, ensuring that the conversation kept on the lighter side of life. Brian didn't even stray into the realm of football when the conversation sagged, an area neither man knew much about. The conversation meandered to the twenty-four-hour hike – something Garrick was increasingly fretting about – and her parents warned him about falling for Wendy's wild schemes. Since childhood, she had perfected the art of persuasion on his sister and father. Only her mother was immune to it, warning him that she was always full of impulsive schemes.

"I've handed my notice in at work," Wendy announced.

Garrick was as surprised as her parents were, He'd assumed she'd told them.

A more serious tone swept over proceedings, with Peggy casting doubts about how she could afford the rent, how a career change at her time of life was silly when she should be looking at pensions and securing her future. Garrick was out of his depth when it came to the loving nagging of a family conversation. He'd left home in Liverpool just as quickly as he could and had never looked back. Then he lost both parents in quick succession, which had led to further alienation from his sister, who he'd always had a fractious relationship with. Then she died, and Garrick had lost everything. A middle-aged man detached from close friends and family, bobbing in the indifferent ocean waves that life threw at everybody.

Until he met Wendy.

As he listened to the paternal reprimands and watched as his girlfriend reverted to teenage pouting and snappy counterarguments, he realised that his life had completely changed. Perhaps it was from watching a life ebb away in front of him, pleading to be terminated, that he realized their lives were entwined. He was no longer on a solo voyage. With that revelation came the notion that he should defend Wendy in her hour of need.

"I can look after the rent," he said with an easy smile. "It will give her time to find her feet."

"You shouldn't have to," Peggy said, annoyed that she'd lost the moral high ground.

"And I have my own house, which I was looking to sell."

"Why don't you live there?" said Brian. "A sight better than paying for somebody else's mortgage, eh?"

Wendy glanced at Garrick, silently informing him she'd told them nothing about his troubled work life.

"I was looking to move on before we met," he mumbled. "And if I do, I might be able to afford to take her to some of those West End musicals she loves." Wendy loved a good musical and had increasingly hinted they should go to London to see more. Not a lover himself, Garrick had been thankful for the eye-watering prices West End theatres demanded. That got a chuckle from the parents and broke the ice.

Only Wendy seemed insistent on pushing her point. "David says it's never too late for a change of pace."

Garrick felt everybody's eyes on him. He searched for a non-damning response.

"Well, uh, y'know. It's a copper's instinct, isn't it? Everyone can change their ways. Even troublemakers like this one."

Wendy laughed with mock-indignation, and suddenly the air was cleared, and the conversation shifted to what she might do next. Her list of possible future careers had increased since they'd last spoke about it, but Garrick was having trouble tuning in. He'd just noticed a text message from Chib.

Amanda Chin had passed away.

THE THREE MURDER victims sat at the top of the evidence wall. Still lacking any definite link, Tim Selman and the razed Dover pub were still being factored into their case. Chib had been reluctant to waste time probing the case, but Garrick remained convinced that Jack Weaver's hunch would yield results.

Dan Summers' picture hung in the centre of the board. The three arson locations — Snodland, Dover, and Whitstable — were marked on a map, with no obvious geographic hub for linking the suspects. The whole team, finally reassembled after months of working apart, all sat at their desks as Chib walked them through the evidence.

"Selman owed money to a loan shark. Dan Summers is scraping a living as a delivery driver and would be hard pushed to lend me a fiver."

"Perhaps because Selman spent it all?" Wilkes suggested, sitting the wrong way around on his chair.

"Then there is no connection between Selman, Chin, and Sajan Malik," she said, tapping the Snodland location. "And the only firm link is that Rachel Summers was working with Amanda Chin."

DC Harry Lord leaned against the wall and swirled his lukewarm coffee as he studied the collage.

"I know you hate this word, Guv, but coincidences happen. At least the Malik and Selman incidents."

Garrick linked his fingers behind his head and leaned back in his chair. He felt his shoulder crack and was sure the whole office had heard it, too.

"You're right as ever, Harry. I hate that word. Sajan Malik is our primary case. We can hardly sweep it aside and focus on somebody else's case like Selman. A case, I'll remind you, the original investigators drew a blank on."

Harry persisted. "And so are we. That's why I think we may be chasing a red herring with Selman and wasting time."

Garrick wasn't so sure, but was in no mood to argue. Since hearing about Amanda Chin's death yesterday, he had felt out of sorts. Stuck in the fog of indecision. It was nothing new. Many cases entered this phase. The worrying thing was that when they did, they were cases that often went unsolved. They could have a hundred suspects, but without evidence, that was at least ninety-nine innocent people whose lives the police investigation was disrupting. People who were suffering unwarranted stress and mental health pressures for no good reason.

Chib indicated a picture of the caravan devastation. "The fire investigation report confirms a faulty gas cylinder exploded, but found no signs of tampering. That's our biggest problem. The fires destroy the evidence. Which means we're back to linking motives based on external factors."

Factors that are eluding us, Garrick thought. He noticed Fanta had yet to speak up. Ordinarily, she was the most disruptive during these debriefs. He was worried how much Amanda Chin's death was affecting her. Should he have a quiet word and offer to send her for counselling? After seeing how his own psychological adventure panned out, he didn't wish that on his worst enemy.

"Back to Summers and Chin then," Wilkes said, breaking the silence. He stood and began pacing the room, his eyes fixed on the evidence wall.

The lad's changing, thought Garrick. Gaining confidence, determined to push his own boundaries. The last year really had left its mark on the team, shaping them all in ways they'd never expected.

Wilkes clicked his fingers. "Who said Dan was driving his van when the bus camera caught it?"

"His supervisor. She confirmed he swiped in and out to return the keys he'd accidentally taken."

"Did anybody see him? Is there CCTV at the depot?"

Garrick unlinked his fingers and leaned forward in his seat as he cottoned onto Wilkes' line of thought. "Let's double-check with the depot. As far as I'm aware, his manager just checked the activity log with security." He wagged a finger at DC Wilkes. "So you're thinking–"

"That his wife was driving," Wilkes quickly interjected to ensure the room knew it was *his* idea. "She wasn't lying about ferrying her mother to the bingo, but there was plenty of time afterwards."

"And Dan is covering for her." It was a flat statement, but Garrick felt they were onto something.

Harry Lord inclined his head, as if hoping to gain a fresh perspective on the evidence. "If the missus killed Malik in revenge, then surely she'd know suspicion would point straight at her? And then there's the odd fact that she and Chin knew one another..."

Fanta suddenly spoke up. Her voice was soft, but it cut through the room. "But Rachel Summers was on duty at the shopping centre the night Chin was attacked. I checked."

Wilkes sighed. "So she couldn't have done that murder."

Silence flooded the room as another theory bit the dust.

"What about Dan?" Garrick suddenly said.

Chib frowned. "In this scenario, aren't we suggesting he didn't do it?"

Garrick rubbed his eyes with the palms of both hands. He had slept terribly last night. After returning home, Wendy had spent hours talking through her future options with him, while he only half-listened. Amanda Chin's death had depressed him, even if that was the fate she was pleading for.

"I hate to say this, but what if DC Liu has a point? Crisscross?"

Chib was perplexed. "What am I missing here?"

He gestured to Fanta. She gave her movie-based theory another airing, except this time everybody sensed a kernel of truth behind it.

DC Harry Lord stated it aloud to the room. "Two arsonists covering for each other. For what reason? For kicks? If Rachel hated Amanda so much, why? Ditto for Malik and Dan. I still don't see the actual connection. And that still leaves dead man Selman in desperate need of a murderer."

"Amanda told us somebody had been to see her that night. It definitely wasn't Dan..."

"So in that criss-cross theory, it would've been Rachel. Which would mean she did both." Frustrated, Wilkes sat back in his seat. "Back to square one."

"Did you know that phrase comes from footy?" said Fanta suddenly.

Only Wilkes was used to her non sequiturs. He shook his head.

"When matches were on the radio. It was the only way commentators could describe where the ball was on the field. They split it up into segments. Back to the goalie. Back to square one." She shrugged, as if it was obvious.

Lord sniggered and swallowed the rest of his coffee.

"Let's talk about Amanda Chin." Fanta rose to her feet and approached the evidence wall. "The cleaning woman who communicated with us using Morse code."

"Maybe she was in your Brown Owl group?" Harry said dismissively. Behind Fanta's back, he had nothing but respect and amazement for her deduction in the burns ward, but there was no way he could be *nice* to her face.

"No, I checked records with the Guides' charity," Fanta said tartly. "I also traced her family in Newcastle. Somebody needed to tell them what had happened, but the trail stops there. I can't find anybody." Garrick watched her closely as she paused for a sharp intake of breath. "It's as if they don't exist."

"Is she an orphan?" Chib asked.

"I'm not sure. But one thing I know is that her name isn't Amanda Chin." Fanta began rummaging through papers on her desk until she found a specific one. It was a printed email from a bank. "The shopping centre payroll paid her salary into her account under that name. But before three months ago, when she started the job, there was no bank account. Then suddenly she has her pay going into it, and the rent for the caravan coming out."

"Who the bloody hell is she, then?" Garrick exclaimed.

18

Suspects with no obvious motives, and now victims with no real identity. Garrick could feel the case was teetering on the precipice of a rabbit hole. It wasn't the ideal time for Drury to summon him to her office for an update on the new round of budget cuts.

"I see the team are all back under one roof," she said without preamble.

Garrick stood in front of her desk, clasping his arms behind his back as if he were on a military inspection. She hadn't offered the chair, and leaned back in her own, clutching a cup of black coffee with both hands and peering at him over the top of her thick black glasses frames.

"Which means I'm getting a lot of grief from other units who have been denied resources." Garrick felt he was on tricky ground. Alienating colleagues was the last thing he wanted to do. "Don't get me wrong, they respect your previous efforts just as much as the folks upstairs do, so they don't have the pitchforks out for you. Yet. Just me." She expelled a weary sigh and put her coffee down. "However, it means that you've become something of an ambassador. Everybody's watching. Some even waiting for you to mess up."

Garrick prickled. He wasn't aware of any negative feedback from his superiors, but he reasoned that there must be some resentment from the way he handled the corruption within the Force.

Drury watched him carefully, easily reading his mind. She nodded. "You should watch your step. Just in case. Remember, you're the one that escalated this from serial killers to people within the lofty offices of government. Between you and me, DCI Kane has gone deeper into the military connections you unearthed. As a result, his department is hoovering up everybody else's budget as politicians, and the press keeps demanding results."

The mention of the press reminded Garrick that he had ignored a message from reporter Molly Meyers. She hadn't pursued him further, so it was probably just a *welcome back to work* text. Learning that DCI Kane was enjoying deeper success, all based on Garrick's own hard work, was galling to him. He was the one who established the link between the notorious Murder Club, created by his ex-friend and confidant, John Howard, while fighting in the Falklands War. From there, evidence had slowly emerged to connect the death of his sister, her fiancé, and several other victims at a ranch in Illinois, USA. As the dominos tumbled, a network of corruption had been exposed to the world.

And for his part in it, Garrick had been given a hearty "thank you", told the case was too personal for his involvement, and been assigned back to the usual grind. No pay rise, no bonus, not even a medal or a cheap certificate printed out in PowerPoint.

Drury kneaded the bridge of her nose. "If it turns out you make swift, conclusive progress, then that'll justify the cost, and everybody stands a chance of avoiding any swingeing cuts."

"So we're fighting crime based on a budget?"

"When has that ever not been the case? Right now, more than ever. The money runs out, then so does the legwork. If you want to pursue it from there, it turns from a job into a hobby."

"Marvellous."

Drury impatiently tapped the table with her long finger-nails and looked at her watch. "Indeed. That's our new world. The result is that we have to funnel status reports up every two days."

"Two days? That's a complete waste of resources."

"Then be thankful I battled them down from daily updates. This case you're on now isn't pretty. Arson is much messier than an old-fashioned shooting. Mass property destruction, endless insurance claims... and I hear we're up to three deaths?"

"Two murders for sure, one death we've sort of... inherited."

"Inherited? You're not running a charity, David."

"Feels like it," he mumbled.

Drury chuckled. "The pressure is on me. More and more people are showing me the door. People still like you, as you can see from that sponsorship form in the canteen."

"Oh, you've signed? Thanks for the donation, ma'am."

Drury leaned back in her chair and clasped her hands across her lap in a clear sign the conversation was over.

"I'm not giving you money for a jaunt across the countryside! You can pay for your own leisure activity. Who do you think I am?"

"A LITTLE BIT FURTHER DOWN HERE," Garrick said, glancing between the map on his phone and the road ahead. "Turn here."

DC Fanta Liu slowed her Polo to a more legal speed as she turned away from Connaught Park and deeper into the pleasant Georgian-style suburbia that surrounded the harsher industrial side of Dover. Garrick checked the address, then pointed to a more modern build, with a sloping driveway that set it back from the more impressive home around it.

"That's it."

Since the morning briefing, Fanta had developed a bee in her bonnet about tracing Amanda Chin's real identity. Garrick didn't know if she was powered by some form of guilt that they couldn't do more for her, or if her own experience of being almost blown apart had left a deep stain on her psyche. Whatever it was, his young detective constable had been more productive in the last few hours than she had in months.

Amanda Chin was a real woman. Or rather, girl. She had died of a rare respiratory infection when she was eight. That had been thirty-two years ago, which matched the age the modern Amanda Chin had claimed to be. *Ghosting* was a common form of identity theft. The deceased's valid birth certificate allowed fraudsters to assemble the identification documents needed to create the legal imprint of a living person. It was a devious camouflage that took the keenest eye, or the slightest discrepancy, to crack the illusion. And Fanta had a keen eye.

The bank account that paid the caravan park rent had been set up from this address in Dover, Amanda's previous residence. Only there had never been an Amanda Chin renting this property. After a little detective work, Fanta found the address on Airbnb and had contacted the owners. They were a couple who lived in Cornwall and had been reluctant to divulge too much information, but Fanta's pointed threats of search orders and a deeper investigation forced them to admit it was a cash payment that had occurred off Airbnb's records. It violated the website's policies, and the owners tried to assure Fanta that they weren't trying to avoid paying tax or commission. The woman insisted on paying in cash for an entire month, and they met in person at the Fleet Service Station on the M3. The rendezvous had been straightforward and the woman, whose driver's licence claimed she was Kirstie Morgan, was more than affable and convinced them she was having banking issues because of an online scam she had been victim to. Access details were handed over, and they thought nothing of it. When the rental period was over, Kirstie Morgan left the property in perfect condition. No mess. No fuss. No suspicion.

Fanta's guess that Kirstie Morgan was another false identity turned out to be true. Other than a valid driver's license, the mysterious Miss Morgan was another ghost in the machine.

The one jarring detail was that the rental period of the property was thirty days, ending two days after Tim Selman was killed. During that period, Kirstie Morgan transformed into Amanda Chin and started work as a cleaner in the same shopping centre where Rachel Summers was working.

Garrick and Fanta strolled past the house, taking in the neighbour's properties. The house was currently empty, and had been rented for short periods three times since their suspect, during which it had been thoroughly cleaned each time by a service company. Passing the house for the second time, Garrick indicated across the street to the home opposite. It was a large, detached building with a freshly painted black and white Georgian exterior. A gleaming white BMW saloon, with last year's licence plate, was parked in the drive. Garrick knocked on the door. A middle-aged man answered, holding a mobile to his ear. He looked Garrick up and down.

"Sorry, mate, not interested," he said, already pushing the door closed.

Garrick held up his police ID card before it slammed in his face. The man paled, muttered a quick "I'll call you back," and hung up. "What can I do for you, officer?" he said in a voice that trembled with worry.

Garrick smiled to himself, wondering what secrets the man was trying to hide. Even the most innocuous incident suddenly had people drowning in a tsunami of self-suspicion that they had somehow crossed the line into criminality. Today Garrick wasn't interested in any of that. He had only one focus.

"I'm Detective Garrick, this is DC Liu. Sorry to disturb you, sir," he said in the most jovial manner he could conjure. "Are you the homeowner?" The man nodded and licked his lips apprehensively. Garrick glanced towards the rental home opposite. "I wondered if you'd seen the occupiers of the house over there?" He noticed a flicker of relief, and the man's body language immediately relaxed as he followed Garrick's gaze.

"There're always people coming and going. I've seen the old owners once or twice. They rent it out and asked us to keep an eye open if we ever saw anything dodgy."

"And did you?"

The man shook his head. "Not that I keep a tab on them or anything."

"Have you seen this woman?" Fanta held up her phone with Amanda Chin's work ID photo on it. "It would have been a couple of months ago."

The man's eyes narrowed, and he craned forward for a better look.

"She looks familiar. There was a woman like her. Asian," he clarified with embarrassment. "But she had different hair. Longer. Curly."

A wig, Garrick thought.

"Said little. Said nothing, in fact. Then again, most of them don't. She was quiet."

"How about any visitors?"

The man shook his head as he thought back. "Nope." He focused on the middle distance as he recalled a detail. "Her car wasn't quiet, though." He caught Garrick's curious look. "Exhaust pipe rattled like hell. When she came back late, it woke the wife up." The last was said with clear implications of just how bad that was.

"Well, thank you for your time." Garrick pulled a crumbled business card from his pocket and handed it over. "If you or your wife remember anything else, please email me or call."

"Sure," the man said without glancing at the card.

Garrick turned to leave, but Fanta remained in place.

"Was it her Fiat Panda?"

The man's forehead crinkled. "A Beetle. Crappy red old one."

Fanta's eyes scanned the front of the man's home, eventually falling onto a security camera keeping a watchful eye on his BMW in the drive and pointing in the direction of the house opposite.

"We'd like to look at your camera footage," she said with an edge of authority that surprised Garrick.

BACK IN THE INCIDENT ROOM, it didn't take Fanta long to find what she wanted. The man had given her the camera's SD card with nothing more than a grumble that he wanted it back quickly. The device had been set to record when it detected movement, and to auto-delete the images after a week. There was no old-fashioned motion sensor. Instead, the camera constantly compared images to detect movement, which meant if a car parked in the drive opposite pulled onto the street, it would record a short video, then delete it.

Luckily, the SD card was a hefty 512GB, and the videos were highly compressed small files. Like most digital data, it was never truly deleted; it was just rendered invisible by the security operating system, so appeared as free space. It only truly vanished when the data was overwritten with new information. It was a simple job for the forensic lab to see what fragments had been labelled 'invisible', but with growing waiting lists, it could be months before they could get to it. Fanta knew that a simple disk recovery program was just as capable of doing the same task. With so much free space, and so little traffic passing outside, Fanta revealed video files stretching back six months.

There were none of Amanda Chin – or the mysterious Kirstie Morgan – but for the month-long rental period, there were plenty showing her battered red Beetle coming and going. The image quality wasn't perfect, so the licence plate was blurry, but not so much that she couldn't make an educated guess at what it read. A quick check on the DVLA database confirmed the vehicle was registered to Kirstie Morgan. Bought fifth hand a month earlier and sold the day she ended the house rental to the website *We'll Buy Your Motor.*

"She had a funky light-blue Fiat Panda parked in Paradise Cove," Fanta said, as Garrick peered over her right shoulder. "Registered to Amanda Chin."

DC Lord sat to her left. "This is some carefully crafted identity fraud. There are only a few types of people who'd go out of their way to do this."

"Assassins!" Fanta breathed.

"I was thinking of con artists." Harry pulled a face. "But, yeah, them too."

"It's not a cheap task to pull off," said Garrick. "What about a link between Selman and Kirstie Morgan?"

It took Fanta several moments to respond as she concentrated on her screen. Rapidly typing one moment, then clicking through options the next, all with such speed that neither of the men could keep up. "I've already... looked. Nothing," she added after a long pause. "I've messaged Sean and Chi... DS Okon to see if we can get video from the dealerships." She lapsed into another long, painful silence as she navigated through the computer.

Garrick and Harry swapped a bemused look. Then:

"Bongo!" she declared.

"You mean 'bingo'," Harry clarified.

She leaned back in her chair, laced her fingers together, and cracked her knuckles. "I know what I mean." She gestured to the screen. "And I had a hunch of who else would go to all those measures to swap identities. And I think I've found her. Gentlemen, meet Amanda Chin, Kirstie Morgan, and Jenny Tengku. A private detective."

19

It was always a worrying sign when a case meandered down multiple paths with no obvious direction to keep it on the rails. Garrick had seen far too many cases snake out of control that way, and now Fanta's revelations, while the only lead they had, threatened to do just that.

By the end of the day, they had established that Jenny Tengku was... most likely... her real identity, and ran Tengku Detective Services, based in London. Unlike other countries, the UK had no regulations when it came to who could be a private detective, and Tengku had seized the opportunity. Her office address was a PO Box in central London, but from there it was a simple task to trace her home address in Croydon, south London.

Garrick asked Chib to accompany him, as London was her old stomping ground. To his surprise, she suggested that DC Liu should pursue it; it was her lead, after all. He caught Chib watching for a reaction from Fanta. She was extending an olive branch between them, but from the way Fanta refused to make eye contact, nor did a flicker of recognition pass her face, it didn't work. DC Liu had made no secret about how immoral she thought placing Chib in the heart of Garrick's team had been. It hadn't been Chib's decision, but that didn't stop Fanta holding a grudge. Garrick just hoped it didn't fester so much to become a disciplinary problem. That would put him between a rock and a hard place.

DAYS PASSED as they waited for the search warrant to come through. Days in which the case made little progress, which gave Garrick time to dwell on his personal life, and just what it would mean to support Wendy in her career change. He wasn't a frugal man by nature, and had a healthy savings pot because, before Wendy, he had little in the way of a social life. Yet, as she mulled between searching for a job or doing a university degree, he worried that this new adventure would rapidly eat through his nest egg. Staring at the evidence wall yielded no further insights into their suspects' motives. Instead, Garrick's thoughts drifted to the idea of selling his house. Perhaps it was the sudden shift in his home life, but Garrick was increasingly of the belief that his old home was an anchor to his past. Something that needed severing in order to start a fresh beginning. The nightmare of discovering Dr Amy Harman's mutilated body continued with this predictable regularity, with or without the sleeping tablets. He hoped that such familiarity would blunt the emotional pain he felt each time, but his mind refused to play down the horror.

He now convinced himself that it was something he had to confront.

"Are you sure about this?" Wendy asked as they stood at the end of the drive.

They had taken the day to go for a coastal walk from Dover to Dungeness nuclear power station. Wendy had wanted something a little more challenging to prepare them for the twenty-four-hour hike, but Garrick's leg was still causing him pain. Despite this, he convinced her he was still up for the challenge. He'd almost convinced himself.

"It's only a house," said Garrick with a forced chuckle. Just staring at his front door was making his stomach churn. He'd intended to make the visit on his own, but Wendy had insisted on coming, and he didn't have the courage to dissuade her. He pulled the key from his pocket and was alarmed to see his hand was shaking. He kept it low so that Wendy couldn't see. "I can't avoid it forever." He sucked in a deep breath, which he held as he strode to the front door. The key scratched the plate three times before he steadied it enough to slip into the barrel. A quick twist and he was inside, muscle memory reaching for the keypad just inside to disable the alarm.

The air was musty and tinged with the metallic scent of blood. Or so Garrick thought. Wendy followed him close behind, but didn't react to any wayward odours as she stooped to pick up the excessive junk mail that had accumulated behind the door.

Garrick looked around the living room. Compared to Wendy's cluttered house, it was spartan. Other than a line of his fossils on the faux mantle, there was no hint of the owner's personality. A critical part of his mind whispered that it was evidence he was a shell of a man, and recent events had enforced that notion. He shivered, partly from the sudden hostile voice in his head, partly from the fact that the heating had been off for months.

As Wendy walked ahead into the kitchen, he reacted

when she gave a yelp. He rushed in, body tense for what he might find.

"I think you left something that's gone off," she said with a slight wretch in her throat.

It took several seconds for the rotting smell to register with Garrick. He zeroed in on the bin and lifted the lid. Inside, a crust of dead flies stuck to the top of the bin liner. He'd emptied the cupboards and the fridge before moving in with Wendy and had sworn he'd emptied the bins. Evidently not.

Wendy opened the stiff window above the sink to let in the cool air.

"I'll sort this out," she said with a faint smile. "You just..." she gestured to the rest of the house, sensing that he needed time alone to decide. She put her iPhone on the counter and selected a Sia album to blast through the speaker as she set about opening more windows and the back door.

Garrick took his cue and, after a brief glance at the dining table where his fossil cutting kit remained untouched, he headed back down the hall to the staircase. As soon as his hand touched the banister, his leg muscles froze, unwilling to propel him upstairs, and the image of blood trickling down the steps like a lurid waterfall popped into his mind. He'd originally assumed it was paint, which was an embarrassing confession for a trained police officer to make. He'd experienced how witnesses often muddle facts and made absurd assumptions while under the spotlight of extreme emotional turmoil, but now understood how the brain tried to soften reality when perceiving something so incomprehensible.

He willed himself upwards.

The steps squeaked and groaned louder than he remembered. With each, the top of the landing came into view, the

wall to the right providing a barrier from the rest of the
landing until he was at the top. A view that had brought
Amy's corpse into focus with agonising slowness when he
stumbled upon her.

Now he was looking at a bare section of floor. The blood-
stained carpet had been removed for evidence, and the floorboards beneath cleaned – although he swore the dark
patches in the grain were blood stains. The wall Amy's body
had been propped against, and the bloodied scrawl, *Miss Me?*
had been painted over multiple times.

Every time he blinked, the words reappeared on the wall.
Amy, with dead eyes peering directly at him, reappeared with
her lips twisted in a knowing, mocking grin.

Only the sounds of Sia, Wendy's off-key singing, and the
noises of her cleaning up brought reality back to the moment.
But reality came with several caveats. Out of the notorious
Murder Club members, DCI Kane's investigation had yet to
conclude who had murdered Dr Amy Harman. No DNA
evidence of the identified killers had been found in the house,
although they had been scrupulous in their activities so as not
to leave a shred of proof. The loose end bothered Garrick –
there were far too many of them. The mysterious woman who
had planted malware on two of the victim's computers had yet
to be identified. His sister's body hadn't been found in America, and the exact identity of her killer remained a puzzle.

Far too many loose ends.

They were a mental itch that Garrick could not scratch. A
tick that quietly gnawed his confidence and self-worth. And
none of it was *his* case. Like it or not, he had to remind
himself that it wasn't his responsibility to solve those crimes.
He was a victim, not the investigator, and like all survivors of

crime, it was up to him to repair his life, not solve the mystery. It was clear the house was a millstone around his neck. It wasn't a place he ever wanted to return to, and his old life was one he needed to leave behind.

The surge of resolution tingling through him was a welcome surprise. He acknowledged that his sister's death may never be fully resolved – it wasn't something that any victim wanted to hear, but as a detective, he knew it was all too common. Accepting that truth suddenly lifted a weight off his shoulders.

He walked purposefully into his bedroom. The clothes and toiletries he possessed had long since made their way to Wendy's... *to his new home*, he corrected himself. The bedsheets remained crumpled from when he'd last slept under them, but other than a pile of books, including an unfinished *Clive Cussler* novel and one on palaeontology, there was nothing to indicate this was still his home. He remembered an empty sports bag under the bed and shoved the books inside. Opening the wardrobe, he found a box containing an old camera, several USB cables, and two photo albums. They all went into the bag. He paused to quickly leaf through the albums. They were ones he'd salvaged from his parents' house, showing old holidays in Wales and he and his sister standing either side of their parents. There were few in which they stood together, and the rare times they did, both children wore sullen expressions as if their proximity soured the air. He ran his finger across a picture of him grinning in front of his beloved fish tank — the very one his sister had poisoned out of spite. The cheap print had bleached over the years, but Garrick was taken by the innocence and hope in his young eyes...

He snapped the book closed and shoved it in the bag as Wendy called from downstairs.

"David? Is everything alright?"

"Yes. Fine. Everything's fine." He assured her. "I'm coming down."

Cramming his bag with the cleaning equipment from the dining room and the fossils from the mantle, Garrick mentally bid the house farewell. He wouldn't be coming back. By the time Wendy had started the car and driven around the corner, he didn't even look in the mirror. Instead, he Googled local estate agents and made a mental list of those he should call first thing on Monday.

A text message from Molly Meyers interrupted his search. She still wanted to talk to him. Garrick considered answering, but instead he ignored it. From now on, he was taking control of his life, and he'd live it on his own terms.

20

No sooner had Garrick arrived at the station on Monday morning, intending on calling estate agents to put his house on the market, then he was back in the car and heading to London with DC Liu. The search warrant had finally come through after navigating the increasing backlog through the Magistrate's court.

Jenny Tengku's home was a modest, rented terrace house close to the centre of Croydon. Initial hopes of an easy entry were thwarted when the owner discovered Tengku had changed the locks during her tenancy. Garrick and Liu waited in a nearby café as a locksmith, overseen by a uniformed officer, sought entry. Liu was uncharacteristically silent and spent most of her time reading on her phone and stifling conversation with single word answers. The old Garrick would have pushed her, but he took the time to book appointments with three estate agents via their websites so that he could get an evaluation on his house. Next, he replied to Molly Meyers' text message and suggested a coffee in Maidstone. After all they'd been through, it felt impersonal to talk in a series of emotionless text messages. He'd missed a call from Jack Weaver, who hadn't left a voicemail, but followed up with an email regarding details of the Tim Selman incident.

"He's still convinced the Selman fire is linked," he murmured to himself. When Fanta didn't react, he sighed and quickly scrolled through the email. During the lull in the investigation, DC Wilkes had delved into Selman's strand and spoken to the original investigator. She'd tracked down the loan shark who had several side businesses and was currently doing time in Dartmoor for GBH after beating up some poor bloke who'd overstretched his financial commitments. He may be a thug, but she was certain that murder was a step too far. He cared far too much about reclaiming his money, and the dead didn't pay. Wilkes couldn't find any evidence, but strongly thought Selman may have set the fire himself. He was laden with debt and heavily depressed. Perhaps it was a last desperate act in which he hoped his tormentor would be implicated. But Tengku's proximity to both Selman and the Summers couldn't be so easily discounted, so the theory hung around on the periphery of the investigation and gave the team something to chip away at. Conscious of the circling budget cuts, Garrick's team couldn't afford to look idle.

It took almost three hours since they'd arrived in London before the informed officer came to tell them they could finally enter the house.

"Nice," breathed Fanta as they entered a narrow hallway that opened into a compact yet light and airy living room. The furnishings were so new and bright that it felt like walking through an Ikea showroom. "She missed her calling as a designer."

Garrick moved to a coffee table with several house-keeping magazines and a Vogue fanned out. "It doesn't feel very lived in, does it?"

"Maybe she was just tidy?"

Garrick tapped the Vogue cover. "Almost a year old." A case of style over substance. Or had she simply been too busy?

A supermarket brand TV sat on a stand in the corner and was connected to a Freeview box. A wide, black framed mirror spanned the wall over the fireplace. Garrick glimpsed his reflection and was shocked when he almost didn't recognise the face peering back. He looked older, and with his fiftieth birthday creeping up on him quicker every year, he felt a flush of disgust, wondering why Wendy had said nothing. Or indeed, why she put up with him at all. He glanced away and scratched the stubble growing over the scar on his head. Since finding the growth and its subsequent removal, he had learned not to trust his eyes. Hardly an ideal quirk for a police detective.

Fanta's voice came from a room beyond an open door leading to the back of the house. "Look at this."

Garrick stepped into a dazzling white kitchen that ran the width of the building. Chrome gleamed from the hob, an extractor fan, and an American-style fridge freezer. Either they were diligently cleaned or unused – Garrick couldn't tell. A small two-person dining table had been shoved against the wall to the left and was covered in papers. Post-it-Notes and printouts adorned the walls.

Fanta was already taking photos on her mobile phone. "She was tracking down somebody for sure." She lifted her camera and hesitated as she peered at the screen. With a slight frown, she zoomed the image in. "Look who it is."

Garrick squinted at a printout tacked to the wall. There were four photos printed by a desktop colour printer on an A4 sheet of paper, so the colours were dark. He switched the overhead lights on to alleviate the shadows cast because the sun was on the other side of the building, but still had to lean closer for a better view.

"Forgot your glasses?" said Fanta, lowering her phone as Garrick cut across her shot.

"I don't wear glasses," Garrick muttered, before realising that she knew that and had, in fact, insulted him. That made him smile, but he was careful to make sure she didn't see.

They were photos taken through a long lens, probably from a car parked at the end of the street. They clearly showed both Danny and Rachel Summers leaving their house. From the scowl on their faces, they appeared to be embroiled in a heated argument.

Garrick took in the rest of the wall. A map of Ramsgate was marked with a red dot on the Summers' house. A job advert for a cleaner at the Westwood Cross Shopping Centre had been clipped out of the Kent Messenger and hung beneath the surveillance photos.

"Well, well, well. That clears up whether them working together was a coincidence."

Fanta pawed through the papers on the desk. Under one, she found a laptop power lead, the rest of which was still plugged into the wall.

"I bet her laptop was with her in the caravan. And I bet that's where we'll find details of her case."

"I'll ask Jack for a report on what was identified." Garrick straightened up, his eyes darting from paper-to-paper, hoping one would suddenly reveal all the answers. "We should check her bank account for payments." He flicked through several more sheets, searching for the name Selman or Malik to pop from the page, but as far as he could tell, it was information setting up Airbnb accounts and research on caravan parks in Kent. "There're reams of this. She was certainly thorough." He caught Fanta's expression. "What's on your mind?"

She gestured to the papers. "Creating multiple identities. Hiring a house for a month, never mind buying a car and renting the caravan... none of this is cheap. Whoever was hiring her must have had a major problem with the Summers – and deep pockets."

Garrick nodded. That had been at the back of his mind, too. "It's safe to assume everything centres on them." He admired the way Fanta could leap to far-fetched conclusions when the team was throwing ideas into the hat. No matter how wild they seemed, there was often a kernel of a solid investigational track hidden in there. "What do you think?"

"Mail fraud?" She shrugged. "He's a courier, so maybe he was nicking high-value parcels?"

"The company would have said something."

"Maybe." She circled a finger over the table. "I wonder how this connects to our man, Malik? Let's assume the Summers killed him, did that mean he hired her, and they were trying to stop... whatever this is?" Garrick opened his mouth to respond, but Fanta was now pacing the kitchen as a wave of thoughts tumbled from her mouth. "But he was broke, right? So maybe she'd hired *him*? Maybe he was on to something..." She snapped her fingers. "It fits with the time-line, right? They get to him, then they get to her."

"This is based on...?"

"Absolutely nothing!" She said it with the same aplomb

as a magician revealing a trick. "But it's no worse than the nothing we have at this present moment."

Garrick leaned against the doorframe leading to the living room. "The probability is that they got wind that she was investigating them. The for the *whom* and *why*, let's park that for a moment." He wriggled his fingers as if physically moving the issue aside. "Maybe financials will shed a light there. I'm thinking about the act of murder itself."

"Obliterating evidence. Property damage."

"Vindictive..."

Fanta held up a finger. "What if we're looking at this all wrong? What if our detective was working for the killer, or was the killer herself and got hung by her own... thingy."

"Petard."

"What's a petard?"

Garrick hesitated. "I do not know. But carry on with that thought."

"That was it. Maybe she was victim to her own incendiary device, or experimentation."

"And the Summers were her next victims?"

Fanta pulled a face. "Even I don't believe that. And it still doesn't explain the Selman's death."

"Coincidence."

"I thought you didn't believe in them?"

"I'm starting to." Garrick glanced at his phone as an email from an estate agent popped up, suggesting a time tomorrow to evaluate his house. "After all, life goes on," he added without thinking.

"What's that supposed to mean?"

He put his phone away and nodded at the table. "It means we'll have to catalogue all this and take it back to the station." He saw that Fanta was ready to interject, so cut her off.

"Budget cuts, DC Liu. It means we all must be a little more hands-on."

AFTER SOURCING some clear plastic bags and carry crates from the local station, they diligently photographed the position of all the documents before packing them away. It gave them time to glance at each file and Post-It note in turn, confirming that all Jenny Tengku's research was focused on monitoring the Summers. There was no reference to anybody else, or who was paying for her services. The only solid piece of information they gained was that Tengku had been conducting surveillance for almost two months prior to renting the house in Dover.

"This is not cheap," Fanta breathed for the umpteenth time as she placed a battered blue cardboard folder into a clear plastic crate. She riffled through the contents as she did so. "These are copies of the electoral register. She'd highlighted their names."

"She's thorough. Trying to impress her client, perhaps?" Garrick was distracted as several texts bounced between him and Molly Meyers, setting up a drink for the early evening. He thought it would be close to six o'clock by the time they finished and battled M25 traffic to leave London.

"You're missing the point."

He looked up at Fanta, aware that he'd only been half-listening to her theories. He put his phone down and tilted his head to show he had her full attention. Fanta tapped the blue folder.

"Why get all the minutia like this? Voting status? What does this prove?" Garrick bobbed his head to indicate he did not know. "It says to me she was tracking them down."

"She didn't know where they lived..." Garrick was surprised by the overwhelming obviousness of the statement. Was he so rusty or unfocused to have missed it himself?

"Exactly. It's as if she had been hunting them down, then found out they lived in Kent. So she moves there and takes photos to confirm they're the pair she's looking for. Then she goes in closer. Gets a job with Rachel."

"She tries to befriend her."

"Yeah." Fanta stared hard at the blue folder lying in the crate. "I just can't think why she would go to all that trouble."

"Or for who, detective," Garrick said with a half-smile. It was enough to telegraph that he was impressed with her deduction. "That's the key to this. Find out *who* – and that will give us the *why*."

The fresh direction was enough to buoy both their spirits on the slow drive back to Maidstone, but there was a nagging voice at the back of Garrick's mind that it all felt a little too random, as if a convenient solution was unfolding before them because that's what they wanted to find. Something wasn't sitting right with him, but he couldn't work out what it was.

By the time they arrived back at the station and enlisted DC Lord to help carry the crates from the car, Garrick had convinced himself to take a step back and focus on the original incident that he'd been pulled into. Perhaps they hadn't found the answers there because they'd been asking the wrong questions.

There must be more to the death of Sajan Malik that he wasn't seeing.

It was time for a new perspective.

21

"I was beginning to think you were avoiding me." Molly Meyers stood up from the corner table in Costa Coffee. She stood on tiptoes as she wrapped her arms around Garrick's shoulders and gave him a show-biz air kiss on either cheek.

Garrick gave a lazy smile as they both sat down. She was wearing blue trainers, which gave her the appearance of being shorter than he remembered. Her red hair was cut into a stylish shoulder-length bob, and she wore a subtle tan that hinted at a recent exotic holiday. As she pulled her hands back, he noticed half her index finger was missing after being cut off by a kidnapper. Evidently, the recovered digit was too damaged to reattach. She quickly laced her other fingers together to cover the scar.

"I couldn't avoid you if I tried," he said with an exaggerated sigh. "You'd find a way of tracking me down."

"That's because I possess skills you're completely missing out on." She lifted her cappuccino cup, which was so large it dwarfed her face, and peered at him over the rim. "You look well. Considering."

"What a lovely backhanded compliment."

"I meant after the surgery."

Garrick raised an eyebrow as he stirred sugar into his green tea. Molly's eyes narrowed conspiratorially.

"Don't worry, I haven't been digging into your personal life. I was just keeping tabs. Out of concern."

Garrick took a sip of the drink. It burned the roof of his mouth. "I'm touched. And alive and functional. You?"

A dark look passed across her face. Since he'd saved her from the clutches of a deranged killer, he'd assumed she had bounced back to life with a flourish. Her on-screen personality had continued to blossom. In fact, he couldn't recall a week in which she hadn't been on his screen. All thanks, indirectly, to him. The greyness quickly passed as her eyes sparkled once again in the spotlights above their heads, but it was sign enough to tell Garrick that she was still struggling.

"I'm enjoying work. Never a dull day. Well... some stories. Like, when I've been asked to cover budget cuts in the police force..."

Garrick nodded sagely. "Now I see. It wasn't my sterling personality you missed. You just wanted some inside gossip?"

"Do you really think I'm so shallow?"

"Absolutely."

She gave a little giggle and put her cup down.

"I like to think of myself as thorough. Why fish for one story when I can have several?"

"Then you're betting on the wrong horse with me. DCI Kane is following up... all of that." He waved his hand dismissively. Their collective hurt and pain boiled down to a whimsical gesture.

"You're out of the loop?"

"I'm headed to the storage cupboard. The little cases where I can't make so much noise."

"That must be irritating for you."

Garrick looked around the café. In the corner, a mother was on her phone while struggling to keep her two young children from all-out war over a chocolate muffin. From her pained expression, Garrick fancied that his life wasn't so stressful after all. He turned back to Molly and smiled.

"It gives me time to breathe and saviour things. Something I should've done a while ago."

Molly nodded in understanding, then bit her bottom lip and looked away. Garrick frowned, but said nothing. The silence that lapsed between them wasn't awkward. It was almost a shared camaraderie.

"How's the arson case?" she finally asked.

"Slow. And I have nothing for you on that one." He sipped his tea again. "In fact, it's on cases like that I wish I had your reporting nous."

"I was joking. You have a whole station full of trained detectives!"

"I think police work and investigational reporting are very different beasts."

Intrigued, Molly shifted forward in her seat. "How so?"

Garrick placed a hand on his chest. "We follow the clues, process the facts, and organise information in a very specific way. Further to that, we have strict processes and codes of conduct we have to align to, or even the most damning evidence can become null-and-void."

"Whereas I can operate like a bandit in the Wild West?"

Garrick flicked his hand up defensively. "Your words, not

mine! I'm merely pointing out we have very different mind-sets towards the same problem."

"Well, if you need any help..."

Garrick considered asking her opinion on how the private detective could've found her way into the mix, but kept that information to himself for now. Instead, he opted for a weaker response. "We'll see. Sorry I have got nothing juicy to throw your way, but your career doesn't seem to need me anymore."

"My career is thanks to you. Well, a little bit," she added pointedly to deflate any potential rising ego. She chewed her lip again and refused to meet his gaze. Something was on her mind, but Garrick would not push it.

"Just thank me when you with your... what awards do journalists win? The Pulitzer?"

"That's an American one, but it'll do."

Garrick raised his cup in a 'cheers' salute. "Of course. Why be picky?"

She was still looking away, staring into space. Then she gave a little nod, as if agreeing with an internal monologue. She fixed her big green eyes on him.

"Have you heard anything more about your sister?"

The question didn't surprise him, but the pointed way she asked it was peculiar.

"No. As I said, DCI Kane is dealing with any links from this side, and I believe the FBI has superseded the Flora Police Department, and they're even less inclined to talk to me, if that's possible. Thanks for asking," he added after an awkward pause.

"What was the relationship like between Emelie and her fiancée?"

The question caught Garrick by surprise. His tongue felt

suddenly dry, and he puzzled over the point of the question. He noisily sipped his tea twice as he pretended to consider the answer. He hoped that she would steamroll in with another question he could more easily answer. Instead, she held him with an unflinching gaze. Finally, Garrick answered with a nervous chuckle.

"I don't know. They were planning to get married. It was their last trip before buying a house." He gently tapped his cup on the table to blunt his nerves. "Why?"

"I've been going through the initial report." Molly slowed her pace as she measured each word. "There are some irregularities."

Garrick couldn't hold back an ironic bark. "Really?"

"She lost two fingers." She absently rubbed her own severed digit. "Found trapped in a doorway. The theory is that she cut them off herself."

Garrick had read the speculation in an early report and couldn't imagine the terror she must have been suffering to commit such barbaric self-mutilation as she was chased from the ranch on that snowy Thanksgiving eve, far from home. A desperate act that was ultimately futile, as her assailant, or assailants, as the current theory stated, had caught up with her and bundled her into a car with at least another victim. They had been driven across the State line into New York where the automobile was abandoned in a ditch, but the bodies never recovered. The vast area around the car was a sparsely populated wilderness. The likelihood of finding any bodies was remote and relied almost entirely on luck.

Garrick knew all the theories, had read all the reports, and spoken with the Flora PD officers who had been leading the investigation. He couldn't imagine what had flagged up in Molly's mind.

"She was escaping," said Garrick, leaning back in his chair and regretting that he agreed to meet with Molly after such a long day.

"Yes. And the report says she was grabbed and forced into the car."

"Where her blood was found in the boot and the backseat."

"And on the steering wheel."

Garrick nodded, but took a few seconds to think about what she said. "Her killer had blood on his hands. Then gripped the wheel." He demonstrated the motion.

Molly nodded. "Makes sense. Except I tried to put myself in that situation."

Garrick nodded, appreciating that it would be far easier for her after recent events.

"Whether there was one of the Murder Club pursuing her, or several, that doesn't really make a difference. If they had her cornered, and probably weak from the loss of blood in her fingers, why would they shove her in a car to escape in the middle of a blizzard?"

The report had stated that a storm had hit the area hard the previous night, making many roads inaccessible. That was what had probably driven them to seek refuge in the ranch in the first place.

Garrick hated to admit it, but her comment had given him pause for thought.

"So she got behind the wheel first, then maybe they wrestled her out."

Molly nodded. "Sure. That's what I would do. I would try to escape regardless of the storm." She toyed with her cup. "I would have locked the doors too, assuming I had the keys. So, perhaps she did."

"That's an interesting insight, Molly, but I'm not sure where you're going with it."

She drummed her fingers on the table as she shaped her thoughts. "There were a few other oddities in the report that just made me rethink events."

"I don't see how it alters the general assumption that she was escaping, and they got to her before she could."

Molly forced a smile. "I'm sorry, David. Blame the suspicious reporter in me. I was just searching for an alternative narrative which probably isn't there. I know what happened to me is tangential to what happened over there, but I still feel I'm part of the mix."

"You are, Mol." Garrick was surprised by the sincerity in his voice. "And none of that would have happened to you if it wasn't for me, so I feel as guilty as hell. If I could go back and change things..."

"You can't. Nobody can. But it doesn't hurt to question the established facts. Who knows what's missing or has been overlooked?"

Garrick nodded in understanding. He felt the same about Sajan Malik. He was sure the answers lay there.

Garrick and Chib stood outside Sajan Malik's home. Both she and DC Wilkes had canvassed the residents yet again to see if anybody had any fresh memories about the night of his death, but the results remained predictably unchanged.

"There is no sign of forced entry," said Chib, her arms folded as they went through the events of his death yet again. "And nobody heard anything out of the ordinary."

"And yet something forced him out of his house in the dead of night. Forced him to run from a place of safety." Garrick traced a finger from the front door and down the road towards the dual carriageway and the warehouses beyond. "Ignoring any neighbours who may have been able to help. Scrambled up an incline covered in junk and weeds – all in the dark. Across the road, and towards the industrial area."

Chib looked at him blankly. "We're assuming he was already home."

"Neighbours saw him come home at eleven thirty. After that, nobody heard anything."

"He could have left earlier."

"Granted. Even so," he indicated the route again, "it's a bloody daft direction to go." Molly's words from the previous night echoed in his head: *an alternative narrative.* "Unless he was running *to* something."

Chib's eyes widened a little as she absorbed the idea. "Or *somebody.*"

Garrick nodded and started walking down the road, retracing Malik's footsteps. After several metres, Chib realised he wasn't coming back, so she quickly followed.

"Was somebody blackmailing him? Did he have something to hide?" said Garrick as they followed the curve of the road.

Chib had memorised most of the case notes. There hadn't been too many.

"He was released on bail after a home intrusion. Rachel Summers' mother. I still think that is a pretty solid motivation for them wanting revenge. Plus, Danny's van was in the area."

The security footage from the DCL TACTICS depot didn't show the face of the driver during the time Danny claimed he was returning a set of keys, only that his key card had been used to access the site. Chib had discovered a gate guard had let Rachel in a couple of times to drop off keys that Danny had accidentally taken home. Rather than wake him after a long shift, perhaps she had taken it upon herself to help. That night, the guard wasn't at his post, so nobody could say for sure if it had been Danny or Rachel. Chib strongly suspected it was the wife.

They scrambled up the incline and through the gap in the fence leading to the narrow footpath that ran along the dual carriageway. At this time of day, it was busy with vans and lorries. Garrick had to raise his voice to be heard. He almost tripped on a broken wing mirror casing on the pavement. He briefly wondered if it hadn't come off when it hit some poor pedestrian walking along this badly designed path.

"Let's go with the idea it was Rachel Summers extracting a revenge fantasy on him. What did she say to bring him all the way out here?"

The body of traffic caused a constant, unsettling breeze that threatened to blow them off the path. Garrick hurried to the pelican crossing and stabbed the button a couple of times.

"If he didn't know who she was," said Chib in a raised voice, "then she could've pretended to be helping him? The court case was due the following week. I bet he would have done anything to tilt the balance in his favour."

The lights changed, offering a respite in the traffic. They hurried across to the industrial estate beyond.

Garrick eyed the remains of the warehouse ahead. It was still covered in white and blue police tape across the plywood covers to prevent access. The other units around it still bore the scars of smoke and fire damage.

"So she lures him over here – then pounces."

"It's as good a theory as any. But with no proof..."

"Phone records?"

"We don't have his device to check."

"A letter? He could have had it with him."

"Speculation, but again, as good a theory as any. So he's lured here. She's a strong woman. I could see how she could beat him up."

Garrick pointed to the warehouse. "He runs inside. She follows. Kills him and makes a run for it."

"Fine."

"Fine."

Garrick ducked under the police tape and fished in his pockets for the key to the padlocks on the temporary wooden door. He inserted it into the lock. "Except... Jenny Tengku."

"Jack Weaver remembered her from the body cam footage." That had clearly been bugging Chib. "An arsonist returning to see the fruits of her crime."

"Only to become a victim of the very same."

"Jack theorised she could've been a victim of her own activity."

"An accident with an incendiary device. Except we didn't find such a device at either crime scene."

"Was Jenny trying to warn him, causing him to be out here – but Rachel got to him first?"

"I like that." Garrick pulled the padlock off and pulled the door open. After a couple of weeks, the hinges creaked with full B-Movie menace. They stepped through. Without the roof, there was no sense of being 'inside'; the blackened remains looked just the same, if a little damper. The smell of destruction hadn't diminished. "Tengku would've been worried about Rachel recognising her, so stayed back."

Chib bobbed her head side-to-side as she worked through the new scenario.

"Logically, this all fits. Apart from what was motivating Tengku to warn Malik, and warn him about *what,* exactly?"

"Details, Chib, details."

"Ah yes. Those pesky things," she said with a smile. "Could Malik have been the one hiring Tengku in the first place?"

Garrick hopped over a puddle as he approached the area Malik had been killed. There was no obvious sign of his death, just a black mass of melted plastic and debris fused with the scarred remains of the metal shelving he'd been propped against.

"Fanta went through the numbers to hire her. It would've cost about five grand, and that's without expenses. That's well out of Malik's league." Garrick surveyed the crime scene, picturing every grizzly moment as Jack Weaver had described it. "Somebody else was paying for her services."

Chib placed a finger over her lips as she thought about it. "That raises two thoughts from me." Garrick indicated her to continue. "The obvious one is that somebody else is paying her, and her own investigations led her to Malik."

"The only issue I have with that is she had plenty of data tracking the Summers down. Not Malik."

"We still don't have her phone or laptop. Who knows what's on them? What if somebody was trying to protect Malik and she could only get to him via the Summers?"

Garrick crouched at the shelving rack and took in the distance from the side entrance Sajan Malik had entered and the front door the killer had escaped through.

"Interesting theory," he admitted.

"My second one is that she wasn't working for anybody else."

Garrick looked sharply at her. "She was working for free?"

"We should look closer for any connection between Malik and her."

Garrick slowly stood, his knees cricking as he did so.

"Chib... that's very interesting. And it fits the situation. Then the Summers, or one of them, discovers she has been following them..."

"And they kill her to cover their tracks."

They stared at one another, both experiencing a slight

euphoria that they may be on the right track, albeit with a complete lack of connective tissue.

"And what about Tim Selman?" Chib said.

"A horrible coincidence." For once, the word didn't sound so bitter on Garrick's tongue.

DS OKON RETURNED to the incident room to rally Lord, Wilkes, and Liu into a detailed breakdown of the private investigator's correspondence, hoping to find a connection to Sajan Malik. With both her phone and laptop missing since the explosion, she warned Garrick that the evidence, if it existed, may never come to light. No doubt that was the killer's intention.

Meanwhile, Garrick arranged a meeting with Jack Weaver to go over his own reports, just in case something had been missed. On arriving at the office at the Maidstone fire station, Garrick was bowled over by the man's enthusiasm and preparation. A large meeting room had been appropriated, and three case files had been laid out on a table big enough to seat twenty. Weaver was sucking on his vape, filling the room with a sweet mango scent as he set up a whiteboard, giving the impression of a trainee teacher trying to impress an Ofsted inspector. Garrick was now convinced that the Fire Inspector was an armchair detective.

Weaver spread each file open to reveal photos of the fire damaged crime scenes.

"What exactly are you looking for?" his keen eyes glanced over the images.

Garrick tapped the Red Dragon pub image. "This isn't connected. It's just a distraction." He ignored Jack's flicker of disappointment. Almost immediately he had discounted the amateur sleuth's primary suggestion. "Let's focus on the warehouse and caravan. The cause of those fires."

Jack licked a finger and cycled through several papers in the warehouse file until he found the relevant one: a summary of his findings.

"An accelerant was probably used, but I think the intensity was because of the mixture of chemicals stored on the site."

"So unintentional?"

"Well..."

"From the forensic evidence, it looks as if Malik made his own way into the warehouse. He wasn't forced there. In fact, we think he was rendezvousing with somebody, but was intercepted by the killer, who he didn't expect to run into."

"Oh? What makes you think that?"

"He wasn't forced from his home. He chose a late hour and met somewhere out of the way so they wouldn't be seen. And now the accidental nature of the ferocity of the fire makes me think that the killer's intention was to burn him so that he suffered, but then things got rapidly out of hand."

Jack nodded and reread his report. "Forcing the attacker to escape through the front."

"Exactly."

Jack's hand hovered over the caravan site incident. "And Amanda Chin being at the fire, at such a late time?"

Garrick was suddenly aware of how out of the loop Jack was.

"Ah, the woman who doesn't exist." Jack's look of confusion made him smile. "It was an alias. Her real name was Jenny Tengku. She was a private investigator."

Jack's frown deepened. "I suppose arsonists come from all walks of life."

"She was tracking down a pair of suspects with direct links to Sajan Malik. He was going to court after attacking one of their mothers. So we have a nice little triangle of motivation – except her role is still murky."

Jack slid the pub fire file towards Garrick. "You were quick to discount this one."

"A suicide? He was in debt to a loan shark who has no connection to the other victims. Our mysterious PI rented a home in Dover at the same time, but that seems to be just one of those things." Jack couldn't hide his frustration over the conclusion. Garrick felt the need to placate him. "Look, you did what every good detective would do. You gathered everything together. Our job was to discount what wasn't relevant. Evidence needs a certain threshold to stand in court; it can't rely on providence. No, we think the two suspects she was tracking down are the right ones." His finger scanned over the case files. "Only we're lacking detail and connectivity. Right now, it's all suspicion."

Jack shifted position and seemed to brighten.

"So I can still be of some use, huh?"

Garrick laughed. "Bloody hell, mate. If it makes you feel any better, you're our primary expert!" They both laughed, dispelling the tension that had formed. "That's why I hoped that together we'd find something we've overlooked in all of this." Garrick clapped his hands together so suddenly that Jack flinched. "Laptop and phone." He tapped the caravan site file. "She must've had them with her. There was nothing in her car or other properties that she rented."

Jack shook his head. "Then I guess they were destroyed in the explosion and fire. It was intense."

"You found nothing?"

"Electronic equipment like the television and microwave

were destroyed. There was nothing identifiable." He popped the cap off a chunky black marker, filling the area with its acrid scent. "Let's work out an evidence wall, then. I've always wanted to do one."

Garrick couldn't hide his smile. Jack Weaver certainly had missed out on his dream profession.

GARRICK HAD to head straight to an appointment with an estate agent at his old home, so called Chib to update her on his conversation with Jack Weaver. Despite an energetic breakdown of the crime scenes, which led to two A2 pads covered in scribblings being pinned to the wall, they had come no closer to bridging the gap between evidence strands. Chib had similar news. They were still waiting for Jenny Tengku's bank statements, but her credit card ones had come through, showing that she had maxed two cards on her investigation, both with five-thousand-pound credit limits. Nothing else had jumped out of the documents recovered from her London home, other than a clear trail that had led her to the Summers.

The estate agent was waiting outside the house in a gleaming Volkswagen Golf. Dressed in a sharp, but cheap suit, Dan – as he introduced himself – looked as if he was still fresh in college, but wore a cocksure attitude that befitted an estate agent, and Garrick found repulsive. Garrick handed over the keys and refused to enter while the young man looked around. He'd already looked at what the other houses in his street had gone for, so questioned why he needed the spotty youth telling him what he already knew about his house and tagging it with a price they'd both found on the internet. But this was the way things were done.

Discontent, he sat in his car and saw a missed text from Wendy who had left work at midday because she'd felt sick. That's all he needed to contract an illness. Technically, he should still be on sick leave after his operation, although he had to admit that he felt fine, and the last few days had been completely free of headaches and hallucinations. He put that down to the distraction work offered him.

He glanced at his Guess black diver's watch. The red inner ring had caught his eye once on some distant holiday, and he was reminded that perhaps it was time he and Wendy took a holiday somewhere warm. With a beach. It was six thirty, but he still made a call to Zoe, his go-to forensics officer. She was a workaholic, so he wasn't surprised when she answered on the third ring.

"Dave!" her Australian accent bubbled over the phone line. "I was beginning to think you'd solved all the crime in Kent. Tell me you've got something interesting for me."

"Sorry, it's the same-old fluff. That caravan fire at Paradise Cove."

"What about it?" He could hear a keyboard clacking in the background as she accessed the file.

"We're missing the victim's laptop and mobile."

"They weren't collected from the scene. Nothing in her car or in the wreckage."

"The fire inspector said the heat would have destroyed them, but I was just wondering if there were any signs they were there."

"The heat would've destroyed the plastic cases if they were PCs or something like a Samsung. Apple gear's a little more robust. It wasn't hot enough to melt glass, so that and the metal chassis would've been there. A regular hard drive would've warped the magnetic disc inside, and a solid state would have melted considerably. The keyboard would be toast, and the solder holding everything together would be buggered."

"So it would be unlikely you could recover anything from the devices."

"Right."

"But their remains would be recognisable?"

"Almost certainly. Either she didn't own any devices, or they weren't there."

After a few more pleasantries, in which Garrick detected a note of flirtation from her, they hung up. Jenny Tengku had mobile phone bills, and the power cord at her London property had revealed she owned a Dell laptop that was no more than six years old. That suggested somebody had taken them. And his money was on the Summers.

It could just be the connection they needed.

They just lacked a valid excuse to search the house.

23

Three-sixteen in the morning.

Garrick didn't know what had awoken him from a troubled slumber in which images of his sister Emelie swiftly receded from memory, leaving only the echoes of a vague warning. He stared at the clock on his illuminated phone screen and listened to the gentle *putt* as Wendy breathed steadily next to him. He'd been worried about her when he arrived home, but she assured him she was feeling much better and would be returning to work in the morning. She only had a couple of weeks left, so wanted to make the most of it. The norovirus was working its way through the schools, despite the fact it was spring, so she counted herself lucky to receive only a minor dose of it.

A noise from outside made Garrick sit up in bed. He quietly climbed from under the duvet, careful not to disturb Wendy, and crossed to the window. The curtains were closed, with only a narrow gap admitting a shaft of streetlight from the pole a couple of houses down. Moving the curtain fractionally aside, he peered out.

There was a figure standing at his car, hunched through the passenger's side window.

Most people would've flung the window open and shouted, but Garrick was consumed by a torrent of anger and ran for the stairs. He was half-way down before remembering he was barefoot, but fortunately wearing jogging pants and a t-shirt. That didn't stop him from automatically grabbing his car keys from the hook next to the door as he opened it and rushed out.

"Oi!" It wasn't the most aggressive challenge, but it was all he could manage post-slumber.

There was nobody there.

Garrick took a shambling step towards his Land Rover. Had the hallucinations come back? He scratched the scar on his head and swore it scratched back.

"Bloody hell," he mumbled in frustration. He was about to turn away when he noticed the driver's window was smashed. It wasn't immediately obvious in the darkness, but the streetlight glinted from fragments of broken glass on the floor. Garrick was about to swear when he caught sight of movement at the end of the street. Somebody was running away.

With a snarl, Garrick ran to his car and opened the door by putting his hand through the broken window and lifting the lock. His hands were shaking as he inserted the key into the ignition. The would-be thief was already at the end of the road. In seconds, he'd be able to dart down the side street and out of sight. He forcibly turned the key. For the first time in recent memory, the aging Land Rover's engine turned over. Garrick mashed the gear into first and shot forward before he had a chance to disengage the handbrake or turn the headlights on.

His target turned the corner ahead. Garrick's engine screamed as he rammed it into second. His mind was becoming more focused, and with it, the knowledge that he was acting impulsively. It was probably some kid trying to steal his radio, but months of being the focus of bad intentions had forced him to develop a victim mentality – and that was not a healthy thing.

He turned the corner so quickly that the tyres squealed across the road. The thief was standing in the middle of the road ahead – his hand glowing. For a second, Garrick thought he was still dreaming.

Then the glow resolved itself into a blazing rag sticking out of a milk bottle.

Garrick slammed on the brakes as the incendiary was hurled at him.

White cracks spread across the windscreen from the impact, immediately followed by a blinding white light as the bottle shattered and blazing petrol smothered the front of the vehicle. Moments later, a wave of heat radiated across him.

The car juddered as the engine stalled. The stark motion was just enough for the weakened, heated windshield to suddenly fragment and topple into the cabin in a thousand burning shards. Garrick felt the heat prick his skin, and he hollered in pain as he tried to brush the pieces off his lap. Smoke from the smouldering upholstery stung his eyes, and the acrid stench burned his nostrils. He blindly groped for the door latch as he inhaled the cloying fumes. He tumbled out, crumpling onto the tarmac.

Every breath was a struggle. It felt as if his lungs were full of phellem. He hacked and coughed, forcing the gunk from his chest. His eyes streamed, but his other senses sharpened. The wall of heat behind him was singeing his bare feet, and he could hear pops and crackles as the fire spread. His breathing eased, and he crawled away from the heat, only stopping to slump on the ground and turn around when the heat dissipated after several yards.

His Land Rover was completely engulfed in flames. He couldn't fathom how quickly it had spread. He noticed voices around him as residents noticed the conflagration. Hauling himself upright, he was suddenly forced back to the ground as his petrol tank exploded. Luckily, he'd been low on fuel, so it created little more than a deafening bang and a scorching shock wave.

Climbing to his feet again, Garrick looked around but wasn't surprised to see his attacker had disappeared.

FOR THE SECOND time in recent months, the streets outside Garrick's new home had been cordoned off by the police and were illuminated in a wash of blue emergency lights. From the side looks his neighbours were giving him, Garrick sensed he'd already fostered a bad reputation. At least this time, the fire engines were on the adjoining street.

His Land Rover's tyres had melted to puddles, and because he hadn't put the handbrake on, the vehicle had rolled between two parked cars – also setting them alight. The ambulance had arrived first, and Garrick sat inside as they applied cooling gel to his skin and watched as the fire engines made short shrift of the vehicle fires. Luckily, nobody else had been hurt, just Garrick and his insurance premium. It had given him plenty of time to run through events.

He'd been targeted for sure. This was no random criminal encounter.

The speed at which his car had gone up in flames indicated the assailant had placed some sort of accelerant inside, which then raised the question 'why?'. Was it a warning to put him off the case? Bizarre, when he only had one set of suspects. Or was it something more nefarious? Had it been intended that he was in the car to begin with, so he'd avoided a murder attempt? Had the Molotov cocktail landed inside the broken window, then he doubted he would have survived.

Any thought of returning to sleep had been extinguished, so Garrick spent the time coordinating the police officers who'd turned up and was pleased when Jack Weaver arrived an hour later. Garrick had texted him from the ambulance, but had assumed he wouldn't read the text until the morning. He was relieved to see a familiar face.

"Nice car," Jack said with a crooked smile. He took several pictures on his phone, then indicated to it. "Your text woke me up. I forgot to silence it. Then I couldn't resist seeing what a mess you'd created."

"Happy you like my assassination attempt."

Jack's smirk floundered as he couldn't decide if Garrick was being serious or not. Garrick bobbed his head, indicating his seriousness.

"Something was poured in the car that made it difficult to breathe when it ignited. The guy had a Molotov cocktail ready and waiting, too."

"Are you sure it was a bloke?"

Garrick paused for a few seconds. He hadn't consciously thought about It, but when he replayed events in his mind's eye, there was a distinct masculinity about his attacker's stance. That narrowed his suspect list to Danny Summers.

"And there are surely easier ways to kill somebody," Jack said as he turned his attention back to the car.

"Unless they're trying to get a message across."

"Or they're just a psychopath." Jack circled the three ruined vehicles, carefully recording video footage as he did so. "It will take a day or two to get results from the lab about the accelerant you think was used." He glanced at Garrick with a critical eye. "But you came out pretty well, considering what could've happened."

Garrick hadn't thought about it that way. Only when he mentioned the word *assassination* did the gravity of the situation really hit home. As soon as his Super was in her office, he knew a phone call would follow trying to remove him from the front line. Perhaps that was what his attacker was trying to achieve? He'd refuse, of course, but that was just another speed bump in his day. That, and avoiding the inevitable call from Molly Meyers when she sniffed his involvement in a story.

He'd be better off ignoring his phone for the rest of the day. And the sun hadn't even risen yet.

DANNY SUMMERS SHIFTED on the uncomfortable hard plastic seat in the interview room. His solicitor sat alongside, quietly making notes on her laptop. Garrick and Chib sat across from them. DS Okon was leading the interview because Garrick was having trouble controlling his temper since Summers had been brought in.

"You were at home, but nobody can verify that?" Chib said in clarification.

"Phyllis was in bed after taking her sleeping pills. A posse of Hells Angels wouldn't wake her. Rach was pulling a night shift in the shopping centre."

"So we'll be able to verify her movements, just not yours."

Danny huffed. "I came here voluntarily, didn't I?" He glanced at his solicitor. "I didn't have to come."

The middle-aged woman peered at Chib through owl-like glasses. Garrick noted that he had upgraded his defence from the spotty youth he had last time. "You had no grounds to make an arrest, correct?"

"We required further questions, and Mister Summers agreed to come here. He had been released under investigation," he reminded her.

Danny leaned back in his chair and clasped his hands together on the table. "I ain't got nothing to hide. And since I had a good night's kip, you can ask away." He gave a lazy glance between the two detectives.

Wilkes and Lord had visited Danny, and taken the opportunity to surreptitiously look around the house when Phyllis had invited them in. They'd been alert for any chemical containers or strange smells, but had found nothing. Contrary to Danny's claim, he was willing to come to the station for further questioning. It was Phyllis who had snapped at him and told him to do it. Rachel wasn't yet back from her night shift.

Chib pushed a picture of Jenny Tengku across the table so Danny could see her.

"Do you recognise this person?"

Danny gave it a cursory glance. "You've shown me this before. She works at the centre with my wife. As you know."

"I was wondering, since our last chat, if you'd had any further recollections about the night you dropped the keys back at the depot?"

Danny shook his head. "I haven't given it a second's thought. It was just a bunch of keys."

"Only nobody remembers seeing you do it."

Danny shrugged. "So? I don't remember seeing anybody, either."

Garrick thought his answers seemed too casual, too well rehearsed. Then again, he was desperately searching for a chink in his statement. Something they could use to push the investigation further. He leaned forward to speak, an act that told Chib he was going to lead the questions now.

"What would you say if someone thought your wife had dropped the keys off?"

He'd been careful in framing the question. It was clearly speculative, and there were rules about leading witness statements. Danny's veneer of cockiness trembled, and he glanced at his solicitor without answering. It was more than a suggestion that a nerve had been pricked.

The solicitor glanced at her client, sensing his shift in mood. She fixed Garrick with a piercing look. "Just to clarify, detective, are you asking for my client's thoughts on a theory, or are you saying somebody has stated this as a fact?"

"I thought it was a simple question."

"My client doesn't have to share his opinion about anything."

Garrick met Danny's gaze. There was no disguising the sudden switch in attitude; a worry that was concealed behind bluster.

I'm onto you, Garrick growled inwardly. He sat back in his chair. It took a moment for Chib to resume the questioning. She looked through her notes, written in exquisite handwriting in a black Moleskin journal.

"You were driving part-time a couple of months ago."

Danny nodded. Chib left just enough of a gap for him to add further detail, as if relieved not to answer any more questions about his wife.

"I also did some cash-in-hand work. Moving building supplies around. Just some casual labour to pay the bills."

Chib consulted her notes again. "For Big Box Builders?"

"Yeah."

"Owned by Stepan Volkov."

Danny wobbled his head as if he wasn't sure. "Never met the owner."

Garrick's brow creased as he tried to recall the name. It tickled the edge of familiarity.

Chib treated him with a knowing look. "He's doing time in Dartford for GBH."

Garrick rocked in his seat. Stepan Volkov was the Russian loan shark Tim Selman was indebted to. Somehow, in the last couple of hours his team had dug up a missing connection. It now moved Selman's death firmly back into the arena. Judging from Danny Summers' expression, he hadn't seen the link that moved him one step closer to a possible arrest. Before he could say anything, the door opened, and DC Harry Lord leaned inside.

"Sorry to interrupt. But it's urgent." His eyes strayed to Danny Summers. "There's been a terrible incident..."

24

The scream of the siren sliced through the motorway congestion. The blue emergency lights parted traffic. And DC Fanta Liu's high-speed driving was a thing of pure terror that had Garrick regretting that he was sitting upfront with her.

From several streets away, they could see the vertical column of black smoke. They pulled into the street so quickly that Fanta barely had time to stomp the brake pedal. The police car skidded to a halt an inch away from ramming one of the two fire engines blocking the street. The smell of burning rubber and scorched brake disks filled the car.

In the back, Danny Summers scrambled for a door handle that wasn't there.

"Let me out!" he bellowed, pounding on the glass

Garrick was already opening his door and reaching behind to open Danny's door. Danny Summers burst out, roughly shoving past Garrick and tripping on a hose pipe stretched in front of him. He caught his balance and stared opened mouthed at the horror that greet him.

His house was ablaze.

Orange flames licked from the upstairs windows, fuelled by oxygen pulled in through the partially collapsed roof. Two teams of firefighters pointed rigid hoses at the ground floor, extinguishing the last of the fire there. With two men using all their weight to keep the hoses steady, there was little room for manoeuvre in the small front garden.

"My wife...?"

"Nobody's come out!" bellowed one of the firefighters.

Garrick rushed towards Danny. Even as he reached for his elbow, he heard the man's anguished gasp and watched as his body appeared to crumple on the spot. Then Danny surged forward, shouldering past the two men in front of him.

"Danny! No! Wait!" Garrick bellowed – but it was too late. Danny Summers rushed into the veil of black smoke. Garrick was brought up short by the wall of heat gushing over him. He inhaled to shout again, but drew in a lungful of vile smoke and was forced back into the street, coughing and spluttering.

Danny Summers never stepped back out of his home.

Garrick and Fanta could only watch on in silent horror as the fire crew doused the ferocious flames upstairs. There was no question of entering until they were quelled as chunks of further roof collapsed inwards. Blazing lumps of internal ceiling and upper floorboards rained down, occasionally reigniting fires – which were quickly blasted into submission with high-pressure water.

Wearing oxygen masks and bright-yellow heavy fireproof jackets, two firemen hurried inside, as the remaining hose continued lashing a fine spray across the roof to prevent any dangerous heat build-ups. They emerged with Danny Summers' body. It had been found on the staircase where smoke had overcome him. The flesh on his face was severely scorched and swathes had turned black and cracked, revealing livid red flesh beneath. Garrick couldn't tear his eyes away as a blanket was drawn over the body. Behind, he heard Fanta throw-up against the neighbour's garden wall.

The bodies of Phyllis and Rachel were recovered. It looked as if Rachel had died in her bed, but they'd have to wait for a full post-mortem to know the exact cause of death. Phyllis had been in the kitchen. Garrick waited until the Fire Inspector arrived. He was a man in his sixties, with a no-nonsense attitude and little patience to entertain the police hanging around *his* investigation.

Garrick's hands trembled as the full rush of adrenaline finally caught up with him. He could see the incident had badly affected Fanta and, after their nerve-racking drive here, he drove them back to the station at a more sedate pace. His young DC said very little. It was as if being witness to such brutal deaths had drained the life from her. As they pulled into the car park, he ordered her to go home and rest. Garrick went inside to update Chib, Wilkes, and Lord on the tragedy.

"CASE CLOSED, I SUPPOSE," Harry said as he placed a matcha tea in front of Garrick.

Garrick wrapped both hands around the cup. His fingers still shook and were cold to the bone. He guessed it was a shock. Shock from his own near-death encounter less than twelve hours earlier, elevated by the Summers' fiasco.

"Hardly," said Chib.

Harry gestured to the evidence wall. "Our prime suspects – our only suspects - are out of the picture!"

Chib tutted. "We don't know if it was them for sure."

Harry's eyebrows shot up in disbelief, so she quickly contin- ued. "Don't get me wrong, I think it is. Or at least her. Even so, what happened at the house?"

"If they had some homemade incendiaries, they could've gone off," Garrick offered. "Jack had mentioned a similar thing may have resulted in Tengku's fire."

"What a coincidence," Chib said pointedly.

"We'll have to wait for the inspection report tomorrow." He stared at the tiny bubbles forming on the surface of his tea as he stirred it. "How did you find out about Danny's connection to our loan shark?"

Chib sighed and sat heavily in her chair. "It was on Danny's CV when he applied for the full-time position at DCL TACTICS. To be honest, it would've passed me by if I hadn't spotted the firm's name in one of Tengku's files."

A wave of fatigue suddenly gripped Garrick, muddying his thinking. The conversation in the room faded to a low background mumble as he struggled to keep his eyes open. The lack of sleep, combined with physical exhaustion, was rapidly catching up with a vengeance.

"Why did she have it?" Even the words out of his own mouth sounded distant, as if spoken by somebody else.

"You OK, Guv?"

He was aware of Chib coming over, but too tired to respond. It was quickly agreed that he was in no state to work. The three of them could handle things, and Chib volunteered to drive him home when he remembered that he no longer had a car.

She walked him to his front door, making him feel like a pensioner being deposited back home after a day trip. The mortis lock was on, which meant Wendy had gone to work.

Garrick shuffled up the stairs and was asleep before his head crashed against the pillow.

Snow crunched as his boots sank several inches into the fresh snow. The light scattering from above was coming down with increasing fervour. The chill on his exposed cheeks was a welcome relief as he was sweating under the thermal layers, the base of which was clinging uncomfortably to his skin. Each breath sucked in sharp, frigid air that cleared his lungs and made him feel alive.

David Garrick could only remember a couple of intense snow-storms when he was growing up in Liverpool, but this was on a whole other level. Not that he had time to enjoy it. The pleasure of the moment was drawn to watching the figure stumbling through the snow. They were poorly dressed for the elements, in just jeans and a shirt top. As they fell, he saw a crimson line drawn out from one hand, staining the pure snow.

He took a step forward to assist, but stopped when he saw the blood pumping from the stumps of her severed fingers. It was Emelie.

His sister looked up. She looked straight at him with a gaze that pleaded for help before quickly turning to a traitorous snarl. She lunged onward, momentum propelling her forward on all fours as the snow sucked her down to her knees. Then she was up and running again, heading towards a car that was heavily laden with over a foot of snow.

Garrick's attention was drawn back to the direction she had appeared. The doorway to a large barn was open, a golden light seeping from within, silhouetting four figures who had given chase.

Emelie had reached the automobile and opened the driver's door. She looked back, drawing Garrick's own attention to her pursuers. They were shouting, although the words weren't in any language Garrick could identify. He could clearly see that they were armed for murder - a machete in one hand, a meat cleaver in the hand of another.

He waved an arm at Emelie. "Go! Go!" he yelled.

She slammed the door closed, shaking mounds of snow loose from the roof. Even through the frosted window, he could see she was struggling to insert the key into the ignition. Her expression turned to sheer terror as her tormentors closed in.

Garrick couldn't hold back any longer. An overwhelming brotherly instinct swamped him. He had to protect his little sister.

He ran forward, but with each step, the snow seemed to slide under his feet. With all the logic of a nightmare, every step forward dragged in back several inches. The snow incrementally rose up his shin...

"Emelie!"

Now he was sinking up to his knees, but pressing forward, willing the snow to give way under brute force.

He saw her pale face press against the side window as she peered at him.

"Davey! Why didn't you save me?"

"I will!"

The snow was suddenly up to his waist, yet he could somehow push through it with the sensation of walking through thick molasses.

But it was too late. Emelie's murderers had caught up with her, hacking at the vehicle with sharp blades. Sparks flew as metal grated under each blow. His sister's screams pierced the wind. The side window shattered as a machete blade stabbed through, ripping through the middle of her throat, and causing an impossibly huge fountain of blood to erupt within the vehicle – staining every window.

Garrick tried to cry out in despair, but he was sinking too fast.

He was up to his neck and descending. Snow trickled into his mouth, choking him. He could only reach out one hand in a last bid for help.

Emelie's blood-smeared face suddenly loomed above him.

"You can't get rid of me that easily, brother."

Then she held a fluid-filled bottle above his head. The rag tucked into the neck of the bottle was well ablaze.

"I never left you," she added in a spiteful whisper.

Garrick screamed as the bottle was smashed across his face – the blazing liquid spreading across his skin, burning every nerve ending with abysmal agony. He felt his skin burn and peel and could hear the sizzle of fatty tissue burning across his neck and cheeks.

GARRICK WOKE with his legs flailing so hard that he rolled out of bed and landed arse-first on the floor.

"Bloody hell!" he yelled into the empty bedroom.

His hands caressed his face, searching for signs of injuries that were not there. It took him a second to soak in the fact he was safe and well at home. It was still daylight. Warm sunlight filtered in through the open curtains and had been steadily warming his slumbering face. How long had he slept? Two hours? Three?

He levered himself to sit on the bed and looked down at his track suit bottoms. He was also wearing a t-shirt he couldn't recall seeing before. When had he got changed?

Checking the time on his phone, he noticed three missed calls from Chib, and a text message from Wendy:

I DIDN'T WANT TO WAKE YOU, HOPE YOU SLEPT IN XXX

Her thoughtfulness always made him smile.

But then he realised she hadn't been home when he'd arrived. His mind was a cloudy combination of half-sleep and confusion. He saw the time: eleven thirty-eight in the morning.

He must've slept right through to the next day.

With several taps on his phone, he called Wendy, only belatedly remembering that she would still be in a classroom. Nevertheless, she quickly answered in a whisper.

"Hey! How're you feeling?" there was a faint echo, so he guessed she had slipped out into the corridor.

"I've just woke up. Sorry... I must have been out of it."

"You were. I got home just after six and you were flat out. It was about nine before you woke up and mumbled something about having a tough day, then rolled back over. I didn't want to wake you this morning."

Garrick stood up and crossed to the window. The absence of his Land Rover brought the last couple of days crashing back. And with it, every detail of the vivid dream he'd had.

"Are you taking the day off?"

"I don't think I can afford to." He pulled at the t-shirt he was wearing. It was too tight – or he'd put on some extra weight. "I don't know how you got my PJs on without waking me. That was some trick."

"Boy, you must've been out of it! You did that yourself before I got home. Look, I've got to go. Glad you caught up on sleep. Love you."

"Love you..." he mumbled as she hung up.

He was looking at the clothes he had been wearing. Now neatly folded on a stool in the corner of the room. He didn't recall changing. He recalled little except the dream.

But he had the niggling feeling that something was very wrong. It was a feeling that years of experience had warned him not to ignore. The scar at the side of his head pulsed with a life of its own, as if his inner thoughts and demons were trying to escape through his skull. He slowly inhaled and savoured the calm gradually flowing through him. He made a promise to himself to call Doctor Rajasekar to check he was recovering on schedule. He suspected that he'd already missed such an appointment.

Recollections simmered to the forefront of his mind... and his suspicions began to take form. He rushed to put his clothes on, but threw them in the laundry when he smelt smoke on them. Fishing a clean white shirt and dark blue chinos from the wardrobe, he rushed downstairs before – yet again – remembering he had no car.

With the sense of urgency suddenly extinguished, Garrick called a taxi to take him to the station. Yet again, the irony that a gleaming new Land Rover, registered in his name, was held in a police pound, wasn't lost on him. He glanced at his watch. The taxi was already eight minutes late.

What a man of action I've become, he thought despondently.

25

All sense of fatigue was vanquished the moment Garrick stood in front of the evidence board. His eyes moved across all the faces – now all victims as well as suspects. His team's casual inquiries about how he was feeling went unanswered, and it was several minutes before he realised that Fanta was also back at her desk.

He pointed without looking at the others. "Jenny Tengku. Chib, you said Big Box Builders was mentioned in her files?" He clicked his fingers, expecting the document to be instantly produced. When it wasn't, he turned and looked questioning at her.

"Chronologically, it was referenced early in her investigation. It's what drew her to Dover, and we think some of the earliest surveillance pictures she took of Danny Summers were from there, but we'll have to do a lot of legwork to match up the backgrounds to actual locations."

"So whoever was hiring her fed Big Box to her, presumably with the specific intention of finding Summers."

"I think so."

"Why?"

Chib slumped in her chair. "That answer lies with whoever hired her."

"Her bank data came in this morning," said Fanta, glancing at her computer screen. "There is nothing in there that indicates she has been paid for her investigational services for the last six months."

"Six months?"

"Prior to that, there was a couple of grand trickling in since she started the detective service, but I bet that's a lost cat/cheating husband surveillance sort of thing." She scrolled through scanned copies of credit card statements. "Everything in this case was being paid for by Mr Mastercard. Maybe her client couldn't afford to pay?"

"Without her phone or laptop, this is all speculation," said Wilkes. "I've made a request with her ISP to find out if she had any cloud storage." Storing files off the computer and onto a secure space on the internet, colloquially known as the cloud, was being pushed by most internet providers these days. It was a handy way to store files – and a God's send for police investigations.

"Maybe she was getting cash?" Sean Wilkes ventured. "If I was worried about the investigation being tracked back to me, that's what I'd do."

"But why wouldn't she put it in her bank and pay off the credit cards?" said Harry Lord. "It still couldn't be traced."

Garrick focused on the pictures of Danny and Rachel Summers.

"Did the coroner's report come in yet?"

"No, but the preliminary fire inspection statement is," Harry said, swivelling to face his computer. "But I hadn't had a chance to look at it yet." He sped-read the official summary, reading aloud every few lines. "Smoke inhalation got Danny. Asphyxiation." Everybody in the room knew that was the first port of call when dealing with death around fires. Few people ever suffered the agony of being burned alive. Most were already unconscious. "Rachel, it seems, was the same. The smoke got to her in bed. The assumption was she was sleeping after her night shift and didn't wake up."

The fragility of such circumstances sent a shiver through Garrick. The notion that he could be fit and well, then tuck himself in a comfortable bed… only to never wake up, was a horrible thought. Most people wished they would pass away peacefully in their sleep, rather than suffer, but he couldn't see any mercy to pass away with no knowledge of your final waking moments.

Harry read on. Instead of speaking, he murmured with intrigue.

Sitting close by, Chib gently kicked the back of his seat. "Harry?"

"Mmm? Sorry, just reading the summary on Phyllis. She was found in the kitchen with severe burns. The best they can tell was that she was tackling the source of the fire. Forensics found high levels of VOCs that hadn't fully burned." He glanced at the team. "Volatile Organic Compounds," he clarified with some authority, even though he'd only just read the footnote seconds earlier. "An accelerant that came from a package on the kitchen counter."

Garrick crossed over to look at his screen. "What package?"

"Too gutted to identify, but the fragments indicate it was an incendiary device."

"There was nothing there when we picked him up in the morning," said Wilkes.

Harry nodded. "In fact, the kitchen was as clean as a whistle. I looked in the garden too. Nothing out of place."

"If they'd attacked the Guv that night, then it stands to reason they'd hide any chemicals well," said Fanta in a tone that continued to enforce any lack of sympathy for the deceased. She stopped short of saying *they got what they deserved*, but the inclination was there.

"So an accident...?" said Garrick, returning to the evidence wall.

"Seems to be," said Harry as he scrolled quickly through the rest of the report. "And since you were questioning Danny, that points the finger at Rachel bringing it home with her, and Phyllis setting it off. Or the old woman was a crazed firebomber all along."

"And Tengku's fire was an 'accident' too," Garrick mused to himself.

Fanta spun slightly in her chair, her hand fidgeting with a pen on the desk. "I don't get why they would try to get you, boss."

"Because I'm an important man," Garrick said with a humorous swagger he wasn't quite feeling.

"I mean, it's not as if you'd stay away. And if they'd killed you, then the rest of us would be working a little harder to find the culprit."

"A *little* harder?" said Garrick. "Your concern is touching."

Fanta tapped the pen faster on the table as her mind raced. "What I mean is, it's not a benefit either way to the killer. Killers. Whatever."

That truth had been bouncing around the back of Garrick's mind, too.

"Have we looked into Tengku's family?"

Chib frowned and glanced at the others, but received a gentle shake of the head. "No. What in particular?"

Garrick was silent as he ran a fresh eye over the faces on the wall. Only the sound of Fanta's pen playing a tattoo broke the silence. He licked his lips as the fragmented ideas dwelling at the edge of consciousness when he was at home finally drew together.

"What if she wasn't working for a client?"

Chib's frown deepened. "Then who?"

"Herself. You said it once before. What if this was personal? We've been looking for links between them all, when it feels as if the only link that matters is what drew Tengku to Danny Summers? That's it. I'm willing to bet that everything else will fall into place when we establish that." He clapped his hands. "Let's get a full background history of Jenny Tengku up on this wall by the end of the day." He started for the door.

Fanta stood up. "Where're you going?"

"I need an education on incendiary devices." He could see she wanted to come with him, but he needed all hands drilling for background information. "I'll be back before five. I want everybody here so we can go through all this again. And Fanta, get more on Stepan Volkov, his loan shark activities, how Danny Summers came to work for him. Everything."

He ignored the murmur of discontent as he left the room. Not that he cared. The case wasn't closed yet. Normally, there were too many loose ends. In this case, there weren't enough of them. It had all been neatly parcelled away.

It was now too perfect.

. . .

"JACK'S NOT ON DUTY," said the bespectacled Fire Inspector, who greeted Garrick at the training centre's reception. He recognised him as the officious inspector who'd turned up at the Summers' fire. "Won't be back until Monday."

Garrick noted that there was no offer of help or any glimmer of recognition.

"You did the report on the Summers blaze in Ramsgate yesterday?" He recalled the name he'd seen at the top of the file on Lord's screen. "Edward?"

"Mr Morris," said the man with an indignant sniff.

Since Morris was obviously a stickler for convention, Garrick held up his identity card long enough for the man to read it several times.

"Detective Chief Inspector David Garrick. I'm investigating a series of arsons and their resulting deaths, one of which is that incident. In your report, you mentioned an incendiary device in the kitchen."

"Yes. My report is preliminary," he added carefully.

"But you think that caused the fire?" Morris nodded. "Only my officers were at the property that morning and saw nothing out of sorts."

"From the heat dispersal, I'm certain the seat of the fire was on the kitchen counter. There were fragments of wires and possible electrical components, which led me to deduce a device was responsible. They're now with the forensics lab."

"But they could equally have been parts of some other ordinary device?"

"Yes. But the lab should be able to identify them." Morris was ruffled, unused to having his theories questioned. "Furthermore, heat dispersal patterns on the floor and remains of the counter indicate incendiary material splattering out." He extended a hand and waggled his fingers downward as if miming rain. "Which is reminiscent of a flammable liquid splashing. The victim's remains showed she was at the heat source. The coroner likened it to a napalm attack."

"That's a very nasty mix."

"It's supposed to be," Morris said curtly. "If it was under pressure, then it could easily have reached the ceiling and ignited that, spreading the fire upwards much faster than usual."

"Are these devices easy to make?"

Morris flashed a thin smile. "Everything is easy to make if you look hard enough on the internet. The ingredients are readily available on the high street so that anybody with a GCSE in chemistry could create a potent concoction."

"I take it you have the GCSE?"

Morris's smile vanished. "I did O-Levels, detective. Much more challenging."

"When are you expecting the lab to get back to you?"

Morris pulled a face. "At least a week, but I'd expect a fortnight. They're so backed up at the moment."

Garrick was feeling frustrated with the man's lack of haste and engagement. He reached into his pocket for his notepad. It wasn't there, so he opened the app on his phone.

"Give me a list of the chemicals you think would be used, and any parts needed to construct a device."

Morris huffed, showing more emotion in that one moment. "Detective, until the lab can report back—"

"Your best guess will do. If you were building it right now and needed to quickly gather the material..."

With another theatrical sigh, Morris began listing chemicals and the common household items where they may be found. Only a few items in Garrick already recognised several that Wendy stored under the kitchen sink and a couple he'd purchased in the past during a very brief fling with gardening. Morris warmed to his subject as he mentally scoured the shelves of the local hardware store to construct the delivery device.

"The key is surprise," he said thoughtfully. "It the device was delivered to the house as a package, then it needs to look ordinary. A mail order item, something from Amazon, a box big enough not to draw suspicion. It's the act of opening it that should trigger the detonation." His hands were windmilling everywhere as he enthusiastically talked through the motions. "Of course it could be on a timer, but a detonator like that is prone to faults."

Garrick finished the list and copied it into an email to his team, asking them to check for any recent purchases from their collective pool of suspects/victims that matched. He added that they should check for any deliveries made to the house that morning. He sent the email and was then struck by an additional thought. He quickly typed it into another message:

CURIOUS TO KNOW WHERE PATRICIA ROYSTON WAS AT THE TIME.

SHE WAS DANNY'S MANAGER AT DCL TACTICS.

As he sent the message, he had a peculiar feeling that they'd made a mistake overlooking her. Before he'd even left the fire department offices, Fanta had called back with information that set his own suspicions afire.

26

Driving the pool car, an unmarked blue Peugeot 207 kitted out for general police use, back to the station, Garrick was swamped by a wave of thoughts. Fanta had jumped straight into a general background check for Patricia Royston. She had no criminal record, and it was simple enough to find her work history on LinkedIn – which mainly comprised of climbing the managerial ladder in several courier companies before landing her prime role at DCL. It was her average social media presence that stirred Fanta's interest; an area where people gave away their most personal information without thinking about. From their pet's names, birthdays, mother's maiden names, favourite places... all standard answers for key questions email services asked to secure online accounts.

It was an innocuous picture she'd posted that caught Fanta's attention. She emailed it straight to Garrick, and at a set of traffic lights, Garrick couldn't stop looking at it.

It was a selfie of Patricia at a club somewhere, most definitely not a work's do, judging by the inebriated look on her face. Her arm was around Danny Summers as they whooped at the camera, their cheeks pushed together and lips searching for a kiss. It was a moment locked in time, cut off from any deeper meaning, but it radiated closeness and affection. While she was apparently single, it wasn't a good look for a married man.

"They were having a fling!" cried Chib as she climbed into the car outside the police station. Garrick hadn't even stopped the engine; he was eager to arrive at the DCL depot as soon as possible to spring their questions on her.

"It could've just been a drunk night."

Chib pulled a disapproving face as she pulled repeatedly at her seatbelt, which seemed to only play out a few inches at a time. "Then why post it on Twitter? It must've meant something to her."

"Spur of the moment?"

"It was posted mid-afternoon. So I would say it was a conscious decision rather than a spur of the drunken moment."

Garrick thought back to the first time he and Harry Lord had arrived at the house. There had been a tense atmosphere between Danny when Rachel was mentioned.

"Remember the pictures Tengku took of the Summers? They looked as if they were arguing." She finally clicked the seatbelt in place. "So was that a bad relationship, or did she know that he was having an affair?"

"If that's the case, how did Rachel find out? Did she hire Tengku? Have we been looking at why they were both working at the shopping centre through the wrong lens?"

Chib looked doubtful. "Then why didn't she get a job where she could keep tabs on Danny and Patricia in one place? At the warehouse."

"Do we know if Patricia is single?"

"She's not married. As for her dating habits, who knows?"

"But a jealous partner could equally have hired Tengku."

"Good point. Jealous enough to lead to murder?"

They swapped a quick look. As old as time, jealousy was the primary motive for crime, and that wouldn't change anytime soon.

Garrick looked thoughtful. "Or he could've been trying to end a relationship. After all, he was still living with Rachel. She might not have liked that."

They both lapsed into silence as they mulled through their thoughts. The fresh direction of the case lifted Garrick's spirits. A breakthrough was just what he needed right now.

Their momentum was almost instantly smothered when they arrived at the DCL Tactics depot, and the bubbly teenage receptionist announced that Patricia Royston had a day off today.

"Do you know where she is?"

The receptionist looked at Garrick through half-drooped eyelids plastered with too much eyeshadow and over painted eyebrows that gave her a fleeting resemblance to a reconstructed burns victim.

"It's her *day off*. I don't tell them what I'm doing when I'm not here."

"Do you have her mobile number?"

The receptionist shook her head. Garrick was about to turn away when Chib spoke up.

"We'd like to take a look around anyway, since we're here."

The receptionist glowered suspiciously. "Don't you need a search warrant or something for that?"

Chib smiled broadly. "Only if you have something to hide."

A junior manager was summoned from somewhere in the building. They took a seat in the reception, while they were waiting. Chib sent a message to the team to dig out Royston's home address and vehicle details. As she was typing, Garrick caught a flash of light, glancing from the silver engagement ring on Chib's finger. When they'd first met, she'd announced she was engaged, but since then he couldn't recall a single time that she'd mentioned it to the team. He also couldn't remember the name of her fella.

"Any dates for the wedding yet?" he hazarded, hoping that she hadn't mentioned it in a conversation he'd forgotten.

There was a subtle shift in Chib's body language as she stiffened. "Not yet," she mumbled without looking up.

Her reluctance to talk was barely disguised. With the chilly atmosphere between Fanta and Chib continuing, Garrick had been thinking of ways he could get the team bonding once more. He'd always avoided social interactions. The last he could remember was Harry Lord's birthday drinks, which had been postponed a few times, and that was a year ago. He'd considered hosting a dinner party, but quickly scrapped that idea and demoted the occasion to a team pizza somewhere. Even then, he hadn't pushed the idea any further in case they agreed. Further hesitation came from Chib's Nigerian heritage. In today's climate, he was overly worried about saying something that may sound offensive. It was a common problem that he was convinced stymied conversation, understanding, and empathy. What went unsaid could make matters worse. He licked his lips.

"Are Nigerian weddings any different?"

She stopped typing, but didn't look up for several moments. When she did, it was with a pained expression.

"Only if you're gay."

She let the words hang, laden with meaning, and expected a vocal response from Garrick. Instead, he tilted his head thoughtfully.

"So it's still illegal there. I didn't know, but suspected. Well, it's not here." He nodded sagely and stood up as a nervous warehouse manager entered reception to greet them. He caught Chib's reaction: a brief flicker of relief overpowered by a wave of pride as she stood up to greet their guide.

Samesh was a line manager and slightly puzzled as to why he was showing a pair of police detectives around. Garrick kept the conversation focused on Danny Summers and told him they wanted to get a feeling about Danny's workplace and colleagues. Samesh was aware of Danny's death and expressed his sympathies, although he didn't know him. He explained that most of the warehouse staff didn't have the opportunity to socialise with drivers. There was a communal canteen where they mixed, but there was no operational need for them to work together. Almost everything was automated.

He guided the detectives around the cavernous warehouse, which was a maze of shelves and overhead conveyor belts that put them in mind of behind the scenes of an airport luggage system. Automated GPS tracking shifted packages around, while minimal floor staff were needed for the final sorting as deliveries were loaded into vans, carefully aligned to coordinate with the order of the delivery drops. Sorting and arranging went on twenty-four hours a day, with drivers having between two and four replenishing pickups her day.

"Next door to this is a larger warehouse. That will be complete in a couple of months and will be fully automated. Then all they have to do is work out a way to get rid of the drivers." He didn't sound happy about the future.

While it gathered very little information about Danny Summers, it became obvious that any relationship between senior management and the delivery drivers would be something that largely went unnoticed.

An hour later, Chib and Garrick left the depot. As they walked to the car, Garrick was thinking through suggestions for food as it was already three o'clock and he hadn't eaten since breakfast, when Chib received Royston's home address. They stopped to pick up coffee and two sausage rolls - both for Garrick - from a Greggs on the high street, then they drove to Dartford.

"Are you sure that's the address?" Garrick said for the second time.

This time Chib didn't humour him with a response. Once should be enough. They had parked several houses down from Patricia Royston's home in Greenhithe, in a street of narrow terraced houses near to the local Asda. The street was congested, but directly outside Royston's front door was her white and black Mini, indicating that she was home. What alarmed Garrick was the vehicle parked directly behind it.

A grubby red liveried Kent Fire Rescue Response van.

He was certain it belonged to Jack Weaver. Now he thought about it, the missing passenger wing mirror confirmed it was his.

Garrick and Chib remained in the car and watched the house. He wasn't entirely certain what they should do.

"If you're right about this," said Chib thoughtfully. "How is this all linked?"

Garrick didn't have any answers, just his die-hard copper instinct that was screaming everything was connected in ways they simply hadn't seen.

"If we walk in there now, we're tipping our hat too early." Chib looked at him, uncomprehending. "You've never heard that phrase before?"

"What decade are you from? I get the gist."

"You're starting to sound like Fanta," he huffed, reaching for the door handle.

"What're you doing?"

"We've got no reason to bring them in for statements. A search warrant will take days. We have to find something actionable now. Keep your eyes open."

He slipped from the car and found himself half-crouching like a cartoon character as he approached the Fire Service vehicle. He straightened as he reached the back of the van, aware that he was making himself look more suspicious. He gave a quick look around as he tried the rear door. As he expected, it was locked.

It could be alarmed, but Garrick could see how poorly Jack had maintained the vehicle, so was counting on it to be just as dysfunctional. He hurried back to Chib and rapped on the window.

"Open the boot."

She leaned over the driver's seat and found the release lever under the dash. She popped the hatchback open. Garrick lifted it up. Inside was a farrago of tow ropes, three hi-viz jackets, stacks of small blue traffic cones, and several other items to be deployed in an incident. He rummaged through until he found a small plastic toolbox from which he extracted a screwdriver.

Chib angled around the passenger seat and hissed at him. "What are you doing?"

"Checking his van is secure. You know what car crime is like around here."

He gently closed the boot and flipped the screwdriver in his hand as he returned to the back of the van. Another quick check around, then he slid the screwdriver into the barrel of the rear door lock. With a sharp gasp, Garrick lifted his foot and kicked the tool's red plastic handle. The aging barrel lock didn't stand a chance as it popped through the back of the door and clattered into the van. Garrick braced himself for the screech of an alarm that didn't sound.

Expelling a long breath, he quickly scrambled inside and pulled the door closed behind him. With no windows in the back, the little light that came through the grubby cab wasn't enough to see well. Garrick used the flashlight on his phone to sweep around the cluttered interior. Breathing apparatus, an oxygen tank, ash-stained jackets, and hard hats were all carefully stored in boxes and canvas bags. A couple of large tarpaulins used for weather protection had been crumpled into balls and tossed inside, where they had slowly unfolded to cover everything.

A black sports satchel, stained with mud and ash, was stashed in the corner. Garrick pulled it closer and felt the weight inside. The zip was clogged with tiny fragments of grit, so he could only open it a third of the way, but it was enough to see a laptop and two mobile phones inside. Gritting his own phone between his teeth, he held the bag open with one and slid the other inside to test the mobiles. The batteries on both had died. However, the laptop lit up as he partially opened the lid. The gap in the zip wasn't enough to pull the device out, and there wasn't enough space to fully open the lid, but he could angle it enough to see the screen. It was a password prompt – and the username was *Tengku*.

He'd found Jenny Tengku's laptop.

It was an easy assumption to make that the mobiles belonged to her and possibly Sajan Malik. He had found his killer. Or killers. Although possession of the missing evidence wasn't enough for a successful conviction; a good barrister would tear apart such claims, especially when a Fire Inspector had reasons for obtaining them. An aluminium flight case provided a seat for him as he leaned forward so he could peer into the driver's cabin.

The passenger footwell was messier than Fanta's car, with a McDonald's carton and several empty health bar wrappers. A mobile phone was connected to the car charger, probably overlooked in the driver's haste to exit the van. Next to it, and very much out of place, was a syringe. Garrick slowly reached for the phone – then froze as the door to Royston's house opened.

On instinct, he drew back into the rear of the van and impulsively tugged a tarp over him. The vehicle gently swayed as two occupants sat inside. The muffled thump of the closing doors were solid statements reminding Garrick that he was now trapped. As the engine turned over, the stereo flared loudly, and the occupants started arguing. Their words were drowned by the music. Not that Garrick was focused on them as he belatedly remembered the rear door was unlocked. He lashed out and caught a moulded handle on the inside. He heaved on it as momentum fractionally forced the door open. He pulled it closed before he and the contents of the van spilled out into the road. He braced himself, and already his arm was hurting as he struggled to keep the door firmly shut.

He felt paralysed, unable to move and expose himself as the van sped up and braked at speed. The flight case he had been sitting on now slid forward, cracking painfully into his shin, and pinning his leg in place. He lost all sense of direction, so instead tried to focus on the growing argument at the front of the van. Words were fused with the music and growl of the engine, but the tone was rapidly escalating.

Luckily, his phone was still in his hand, so with his thumb, he navigated through to his texts and sent one to Chib. He assumed she'd be discreetly following, but wanted to make sure. There was no reason to pull the van over. Discovering a stowaway police detective had illegally broken in would only damage their case. Next, he accessed his Google Maps app and waited for it to lock on his GPS location. They had just pulled onto the M20 and were heading east. Chib answered his text moments later. She was several cars behind.

Now there was nothing Garrick could do but hide and pray that he wouldn't be caught.

27

The motion of the map was having a soporific effect on Garrick as the van headed towards Maidstone. The argument had peaked, then descended into silence as they arrived at the Fire Training Centre. The engine was kept running as the driver left, but Garrick didn't dare sneak out. Silence from the passenger eventually provoked him to carefully lift the tarp and peek out.

Patricia Royston's head was leaning against the passenger window. Garrick's first reaction was that she was dead. That assumption was put paid to by the gentle rise and fall of her chest. The argument must've been enough to exhaust her. Beyond the dirty windshield, night was quickly falling, hastened by black clouds that brought fat raindrops smattering against the glass.

The sudden opening of the driver's door caused him to jump. He caught Jack Weaver's profile as he leaned in and watched Patricia sleep for a moment before he lifted a small box inside, placing it on the seat between them.

Garrick carefully pulled the tarp over his head as Jack

climbed in. Window wipers squeaked into action, and they pulled away. Garrick returned to his phone to monitor their progress. He'd been so intently watching the dot that represented their position that he failed to notice the battery indicator was in the red. Seconds later, his phone abruptly powered down. He pocketed his phone and silently swore to himself. Now he was truly riding blind.

The fluorescent dots on his watch informed him it was another thirty-five minutes before they parked again. This time the engine stopped, and he held his breath to listen for any extraneous sounds outside. A mechanical whirling sounded like a shutter rising.

Jack got out of the van, slamming the door behind him. Moments later, the vehicle rocked as Patricia left too, but she didn't close the door. Still, not a further word was exchanged between them.

Minutes stretched by. Garrick was becoming antsy, and the silence outside wasn't helping. He pulled the sheet away and was greeted by darkness. There was some ambient light, and his eyes were already adjusted. He could make out vague dark forms around him, and the faint bumped texture of the open flight case crushing his leg. Moving as silently as he could, he sat upright and peered over the seats. The world beyond the windscreen was dark, with no signs of life.

Gritting his teeth, he slid the flight case off his shin. It had grazed the flesh through his chinos, and flecks of blood seeped through. He was about to close the case and set it upright when he noticed that it contained a pair of thermal imaging goggles tightly packed in a foam tray. He carefully extracted them. He couldn't make out the detail, but his fingers combed the surface and touched a small square sliding switch. He pushed it forward and the inside of the goggles illuminated with the faintest of electrical whines. Through them he could see the interior of the van picked out in blue, black, and grey shades. He turned them off and strapped the elastic strap around the back of his head, bracing the device against his forehead. He gently pushed at the rear door. It swung open with a faint squeal.

The air in the volume beyond was still, yet he could hear the faint drumming of rain. He was inside. He slowly stepped out, his feet brushing the smooth concrete. It took a moment for his eyes to adjust further.

He was surrounded by large shelves that stretched thirty feet above him. Light was coming through skylights in the flat rooftop overhead, which provided a sounding board for the rain. Even in the darkness he could make an educated guess he was inside DCL Tactics' new warehouse extension. What had brought them here?

The van was parked head-first in a concrete bay. Its front bummer was up against the raised concrete loading dock, designed to be level with the back of the delivery trucks. The shuttered door was closed behind it, with the words BAY 9 written on the wall overhead.

He strained to listen and wondered where Chib was. Outside, waiting for his signal? Or had Jack realised he'd been followed and managed to lose her? Garrick shooed the thought away. Paranoia wasn't useful in these circumstances; and he had to believe she had his back as she'd done in the past.

There were sounds of movement from deeper within the aisles. Something being dragged on the smooth floor and the gentlest brush against metal. He was about to step away from the van when police instinct got the better of him. No matter what, he had to preserve evidence. He reached into the van and, after blindly patting around the tarpaulin sheets, found the handles of the sports satchel containing the victims' laptop and mobiles. He zipped it closed and slung the straps over his shoulder. Then he clambered onto the raised concrete dock, his shin smarting painfully as he did so. He took a couple of steps towards the noise, then stopped when he remembered the thermal imaging goggles on his forehead.

He slid the device across his eyes. The screen inside acted like a blindfold, plunging him into utter pitch black. His fingers gently ran across the side of the headset until he found the toggle and clicked it forwards.

With a low electrical whine, the screen lit up in front of his eyes in a palette of blacks and blues. He caught his balance as the world slowly expanded to the limit of the device's cameras, about two hundred feet. Beyond that was a wall of blackness that resolved itself an inch at a time as he stepped forward.

The racks of shelves appeared as fuzzy blue shapes against the darker cobalt of the surrounding air. There was enough resolution to define shapes, but not texture or detail. Black cables hung from the ceiling or ran across the floor like black snakes. The roof was just within range, with the light from the skylights showing as bright white oblongs.

The strap didn't cover his ears, so he could still discern the movement somewhere within the warehouse. He moved his head slowly left and right, taking a few more steps into the darkness, and with it came increasing confidence to navigate around the blue-black cold thermal world. He carefully stepped over cables before he could stumble on them. He approached a narrow aisle between a pair of towering metal racks that stretched thirty feet or more to the ceiling.

He suddenly froze as somebody stepped across the aisle ahead of him. He could see it was Jack, but the goggles revealed him as a glowing being made of pure radiant energy. A soft whirl of warm reds and oranges, as if he'd been constructed from glowing clay before the final details could be added. A deep red spot burned on his forehead. There was just enough resolution in the image for Garrick to make out the square housing of a small head-mounted battery lamp. Jack was holding a metal canister with both hands, dripping the contents along the floor behind him. He hadn't seen Garrick – perhaps he was just beyond the range of his head torch's beam.

Jack moved behind the shelves, but his thermal signature was bright enough for Garrick to see him move towards a figure on the floor. A woman – slumped face-down, but alive with the heat of life. There was no doubt it was Patricia Royston, but any thoughts of collusion between the two were shattered when Jack poured the liquid over her. She didn't react; she was out cold.

Garrick thought back to the van. She had both sat inside and argued with Jack before eventually lapsing into silence. Then there was the syringe on the dash. Jack must've sedated her. Had he done the same to his other victims just before immolating them?

Garrick remained frozen in position. This time his inaction was caused by a crippling wave of indecision. He had never coped well around fire. His life-and-death struggle with John Howard had left him unconscious in the snow until Chib had dragged him to safety. When he and Fanta had broken into a suspect's house, they had triggered a booby trap that resulted in a terrible explosion. But this was different. On both of those occasions, the threat had been to his own life – now he had minutes, or maybe seconds, to prevent murder.

Garrick wasn't a natural fighter. His style was more barroom brawl, but he could generally handle himself. However, Jack Weaver was a whole different prospect. Powerful, fit, and obviously in possession of a merciless streak, there was no way Garrick could take him on in a fair fight. So he had to make the fight an unfair one.

He carefully placed the satchel down and looked around for a weapon. The shelves were bare, and construction workers had diligently tidied away their equipment in order to comply with health and safety mandates.

He could dash back to the van hoping to find something there, or he could try to open a shutter to call for help – on the assumption Chib had arrived and was waiting with reinforcements. But both options would alert Jack to his presence, and the time involved would be enough to light a match and end a life.

Garrick was stuck. He had to work out a way to be the weapon himself.

Walking almost on tiptoes to minimise noise, he stepped closer to the back of the shelving rack that towered over Jack and Patricia. Drawing closer, he could hear Jack muttering to himself. He couldn't make out the words, but the emotion was clear between sobs of anguish. Reaching the edge of the shelving, Garrick gripped the vertical posts, placed his right knee on the lower shelf, and slowly raised himself. Jack was making enough noise to mask the gentle creak as the steel buckled under Garrick's weight. With the shelves a generous four feet apart, it was a stretch to haul himself onto the second shelf. He was thankful that the thermal goggles disguised the depth increasing below him. Heights were another of his pet hates, which didn't help his impulsive plan of action.

Between sobs, Jack's words rose to greet Garrick. "This is your fault. You brought this on yourself, you stupid bitch..." His words were lost in a deep sob.

Garrick pulled himself up to the next level and peered over the edge. He was directly above them. Only twelve feet over the dark blue hue of the concrete floor, it still felt far too high. Patricia's leg started to slowly move, and her fingers flex as she regained consciousness.

Jack crouched to speak to her. "Too little, too late," he hissed.

Garrick's heart was pounding in his chest as Jack put the canister down and reached into his jean's pocket. Garrick swung his legs over the shelf. Unarmed, *he* had to become the weapon.

He jumped down.

Creaking metal caused Jack to look up at the very last moment. The beam from his flashlight struck the sensitive camera on Garrick's goggles – lighting up the screen inside with bright white light. He was blinded as his knees struck Jack. One cracked across the top of his skull, the other pile-driving into his collar bone with such force it broke with a terrible snap.

Jack Weaver collapsed backwards, pitching Garrick side-ways. Weaver grunted as Garrick's body weight expunged the air from him, breaking several ribs in the process. Instinctively, Garrick wrapped his arms around his head. Just in time, as he rolled from the man and sprawled across the unyielding floor. Acrid smelling liquid splashed across his hands and arms as he sprawled facedown and headbutted the ground. The goggles saved him from a fractured skull as the outer plastic casing shattered, exposing fragments of its electronic guts.

A moment of calm descended, broken by pained whimpering from both Garrick and Jack, and murmuring from Patricia as she realized what was going on. The blistering whiteout that had consumed Garrick's vision slowly faded as he readjusted to the darkness. Jack's headlight had been knocked off, and now lay at an angle backlighting the Fire Inspector as he clutched his broken shoulder, and glimmering across the path of liquid he had poured over Patricia, and towards a steel enclosure a dozen yards away that housed several metal acetylene canisters used for welding.

Patricia pushed herself upright, but swayed uneasily.

"Run..." Garrick could barely get the words out.

She looked blankly at the liquid on her hand... then realised that her clothes were sodden with it. Even in the dim light, Garrick could see her incomprehension.

"Patricia, run!" he wheezed. He rolled to his knees. A pain jarred through his shoulder. A quick feel told him it was dislocated rather than broken.

Jack rolled to his side and glared accusingly at Garrick. Each breath came with a fierce stabbing pain in his chest. One arm lay limp across the floor, but he crossed the other over his waist to reach into his opposite pocket. Garrick knew the match or lighter to ignite the liquid was there. It was an awkward manoeuvre, but it was buying Garrick a little more time.

"RUN!" he bellowed at Patricia – at the same time he clambered to his feet.

His sudden movement startled the still confused woman. She slowly stood – only to look up and see Garrick half-staggering, half-running towards her like a drunk. "GET OUT!"

He shouldered into her with his dislocated limb, sending white-hot pain through his chest. Bursts of light peppered his vision to accompany the agony. The metal shelf took the brunt of the impact, but he'd caught Patricia just enough to propel her into motion. She took several steps away from the wet slug-like trail Jack had laid.

A fresh wind of energy flooded through Garrick. He spun around to face Jack – in time to see him draw a cigarette lighter from his pocket. Lying on his broken arm, he held it aloft.

Garrick's legs felt leaden as he ran to stop him.

All it took was a single click.

Time slowed to a crawl as the golden flame bobbed at the tip of the lighter. It was a small point of light in the void. But so was the Big Bang.

With astonishing speed, a wave of blue fire rippled across his fingers. Down his arm. His sodden shirt erupted in golden illumination, and the flame ignited the river of liquid he was lying in.

Garrick pitched himself to the right, attempting to gain as much air between him and the liquid he was standing in. He felt the rush of heat as the fire spread towards him – but with his feet clear, he avoided being set alight. The path of fire continued to where Patricia had been lying and licked at the metal canister. What accelerant was still inside, instantly caught in a fierce explosion that splattered liquid fire across the empty shelves.

That happened by the time Garrick landed on his side and rolled three feet to a halt. He was just in time to see the horrific spectacle of Jack Weaver writhing in a veil of flames. His legs and good arm thrashed, and he let out a constant high-pitch wail. Fire melted the skin on his cheeks. Garrick couldn't peel his eyes away as flesh bubbled and peeled to reveal the bone beneath. The heat popped Jack's right eyeball, sending a bubbling trail of gel down his charring nose.

And still he screamed.

Seconds later, the opposite end of the fire trail reached the Acetylene tanks.

Garrick stood and took a step towards Jack, intent on trying to help – before stopping himself. He was covered in flammable liquid, and any closer to the flames risked combustion. With a last look at Jack Weaver's act of self-immolation, Garrick turned and ran for the exit, praying that Patricia was conscious enough to do the same.

The wall of fire now provided a soft golden glow, enough to spot the sports satchel he had dumped in the aisle. He snatched it by the handles and didn't stop running.

The van was ahead, and he was relieved to see Patricia was already at the shutter, pounding on it to open. Garrick ran for the front of the van.

"Stand back!" he yelled as he jumped inside the open passenger door and shuffled into the driver's seat, throwing the satchel in the back as he did. Jack had left the keys in the ignition for a hasty escape. Garrick turned the engine over just as the Acetylene tanks erupted.

He saw ten pressurised canisters fire upwards at different angles, like missiles. The pressure wave from the explosion shattered the skylights above and cracked the van's windshield into a tight mass of white cracks, as if smothered in a spider's web. Even in the van, Garrick's ears felt as if he'd been submerged in water, and his hearing was reduced to nothing but low, dull bass sounds.

Glancing in the one good side-mirror, he saw Patricia had

heeded his warning and stood aside, shielded from the explosion by the van. He yanked the gear stick in reverse and mashed the accelerator. He drove into the shutter at speed. There wasn't enough force to tear the metal; instead, the entire shutter mechanism was torn from the wall as Garrick reversed outside. The shutter twisted as it cocooned the back of the van before catching under the wheels. Being rear-wheel driven, the vehicle lost traction on the road and skidded in a neat one-hundred-and-eighty degrees on the now rain-slick loading area. The engine stalled.

Garrick winced in pain as he opened the driver's door and almost fell out in his haste to run back for Patricia. She staggered from the warehouse, lit from behind by a growing wall of fire that looked as if Hades had come to claim Jack Weaver personally.

She fell into Garrick's arms. He intended to be the dashing hero and hold her tight – but with one dislocated shoulder and bruised ribs; she slipped from his grasp and collapsed in a heap at his feet. She was alive, and that was all that counted.

DCI Garrick felt like joining her on the ground. It hurt when he twisted around to see a wall of blue lights speeding across the depot car park towards him. Chib was parked to the side, with a dozen marked police cars and an ambulance. She also had the foresight to summon a fire engine, although Garrick doubted that the single appliance would make much of a dent in the flames crossing the depot roof, igniting the main building behind.

Whatever Jack Weaver's motives were, he had made a last destructive mark on the world.

28

E very step hurt.

Garrick sucked in a breath... and that hurt, too. He was only eight hours into the twenty-four-hour hike, and he felt like dying. It had only been three days since Jack Weaver's dramatic suicide, and he had all the motive in the world to refuse to accompany Wendy on this foolish endeavour. He'd considered it too until he found that his sponsorship form in the canteen had reached £1100 because of a last-minute sympathy rally. His fellow officers appreciated a colleague doing well, but they much preferred it if success came with a huge amount of pain; and Garrick was at the top of the leader board when it came to physical punishment.

Wendy squeezed his hand as they walked together. They had started the walk with a dozen faces Garrick didn't know, and most of the familiar ones from their rambling group had been ahead for hours, led onward by Mike and Stu. He had told Wendy to go ahead, but she refused and assured him they were in it together. From the moment he'd returned home after an all-too familiar jaunt to the hospital to have his arm popped back into place, and several stitches applied to his new collection of cuts and bruises, Wendy had been unusually subdued. As the days passed, she seemed to go quieter, unable to talk to him. Garrick felt the echoes of history claw at him. Previous relationships that had seemed strong suddenly crumbled when the real dangers of his job revealed themselves. It was one thing fancying a man in uniform who courted danger – but unlike his youth, he was sans-uniform and a magnet for harm. He could tell Wendy was having serious doubts about their future, and that depressed him.

With a deep sigh, he forced his attention to the beautiful view ahead. The rolling hills were dotted with trees in their first-flush of spring blossom. The azure sky didn't have a cloud in it, and it was warm with a gentle breeze balancing the temperature. If not for his pain and doubts, it could have been a perfect day.

Trying to channel the physical discomfort jolting every part of his body, Garrick's mind slipped back to the case. Even with Patricia Royston in custody, there were too many confusing loose ends. As they were lacking support staff, he let Molly Meyers have access to the investigation on condition nothing was released until the right time, although she'd have exclusivity on the story. Through her own channels, she had uncovered key information.

Eleven arson attacks around Newcastle had the same hallmarks of Jack Weaver. They were expensive property attacks, but appeared to be random. At five of them, Weaver had been the Fire Inspector, a position that had allowed him to manipulate and conceal evidence – not that he had left anything that could lead back to him.

Molly had discovered that his single mother was killed in a house fire when he was twelve. The cause was a chip pan blaze. It was a time when the average house regularly boiled a pan of oil on the hob, risking life and limb for the perfect chip. Everybody on the team suspected that Weaver had caused the fire himself, but at the time, he was never a suspect.

In retrospect, Weaver clearly had a fascination with fire, a definite fire starter with pyromania tendencies. All of which could easily be hidden in plain sight because of his job.

It was at a fire in a green grocer's shop, in the suburb of Adamstown Heights, that claimed the first verifiable murder when the owner was killed. Frank Tengku, Jenny Tengku's father.

That had led Jenny Tengku on a personal quest to track the arsonist down.

The death motivated Jack Weaver to leave Newcastle, and he headed to the Kent Fire Service. As far as the team could tell, he started no more fires. Perhaps he was trying to wean himself off his compulsion. With the killer now nothing more than a pile of charred bones, they would never know.

He met Patricia Royston at the Coyotes nightclub in Gillingham. They'd intensely dated for two years, but never crossed the line to move in together, nor did they talk about engagement or other hints that indicated the relationship was on track.

With Patricia adding to the narrative, inconstancies in the story quickly appeared. Fanta and Chib seized on them like bulldogs, both convinced that Weaver had indoctrinated her with his pyromania. It was a claim she furiously denied, but not one the investigation could easily discount.

While they were together, Weaver restarted his arson

attacks. Molly Meyers uncovered four unsolved local incidents that fitted his profile. The attack on Tom Selman was the next one that led to a fatality.

Circling back to the other incidents in Newcastle and around Kent, the team — guided by Molly's insight — discovered that at each location, the victim had been charged with a crime. No matter how minor, it suddenly appeared that Jack Weaver fancied himself as some sort of vigilante. Garrick's thoughts on how Weaver would've made a good detective, was suddenly very insightful. If he had been responsible for his mother's death, then perhaps it was a self-imposed punishment? Now he was dead, there would be many questions left unanswered.

Tengku's father had the misfortune of driving without insurance while being involved in an accident. Luckily, nobody was killed, but it resulted in a heavy fine and a four-year driving ban. For whatever reason, it caught Weaver's attention and eventual punishment.

While Weaver continued his activities in Kent, Jenny Tengku's self-financed investigation found the clues she needed to track her mysterious arsonist. All thanks to Sajan Malik.

Sajan Malik was a small-time crook. A man who steered away from violence but habitually seized even the tiniest opportunity to make a quick quid. So it was that he did cash-in-hand jobs for Stepan Volkov, loan shark and owner of Big Box Builders. Malik did whatever bone the self-styled mobster would throw his way. From making sure couriers were paid in untraceable little brown envelopes, such as Danny Summers, through to turning up to intimidating late-payers, such as Tim Selman.

The webs had been laid; the connections were all there,

but bringing them to light in just under three days required looking at every angle in a different way, that included a third element: good old-fashioned lust.

Patricia Royston was tiring of her relationship with Jack Weaver. While she admitted that he was a dreamy physical catch, she found him uninspiring and plain dull. She met Danny Summers when he was working part time as a courier. A chance encounter in the staff canteen had led to a passionate affair. Under interview, she took delight in a talking about their sexual exploits in the warehouse and even under Rachel Summers' nose. Things between them quickly became serious.

And Jack Weaver was beginning to suspect she was having an affair.

And that was at the heart of the connections that led to the subsequent deaths. All seemingly unconnected people drawn together towards their fates.

Sajan Malik was tasked by his boss to watch Tim Selman's movements, just in case he tried to make a run from his debts. He'd seen Danny Summers arrive with building supplies for the pub's extension, supplies it turned out came from Big Box Builders. Stepan Volkov was canny enough to ensure that if he was loaning Selman money, he'd see it come back to him in more ways than one.

It was a chance encounter online that brought Jenny Tengku into Sajan Malik's world. With access to her laptop, the team found that she had been posting on social media and message boards, appealing for any information on arson attacks around the country. Sajan Malik had one such incident – the razing of a patch of land that contained four storage containers for Big Box Builders. An attack that nobody within the local criminal fraternity would dare have conducted. This arson attack had evaded the team's inspection because it was never reported as one. Stepan Volkov was in no rush to court police attention. The Fire Inspector was Jack Weaver, whose report concluded that it was an electric fault that had caused the blaze.

But Stepan Volkov knew better than that. He felt targeted, and rightly so when evidence from handwritten notebooks in Weaver's flat revealed Volkov was on his vigilante hit list after he discovered just who he was. His attack on Volkov may have continued if the Russian hadn't been finally arrested and incarcerated for GBH. That probably saved Volkov's life and set Weaver looking for other potential associates.

That had led him to Tim Selman.

Seeing Big Box drivers delivering to the pub, and a little digging around that showed Selman was in debt and possessed a criminal record, was all the evidence Jack required for a revenge attack. Whether he'd intended to kill Selman was unanswerable, although from the way he'd been laid across the bar, the investigators concluded that he may have been tranquilised, as Waver had done to Patricia Royston, which meant that the vigilante was seeking further kicks by resorting to murder.

For the ever-paranoid Malik, this was one step too far. Subtle investigation from Molly and her impressive network of underground contacts quickly revealed that Volkov and his affiliates were convinced that they were being targeted. As Danny Summers was the only connection Malik had seen between his boss and Selman, he suspected that Summers was the arsonist. A mistake that would lead to several deaths.

A quick exchange online with Jenny Tengku had led her to Dover. The private notes on her laptop revealed that she never met Malik in person, but he'd given her enough information to identify the Big Box driver, Danny Summers. She'd taken it upon herself to watch him closely while maintaining an active online exchange with Malik.

Tengku had stumbled on the arsonist's penchant for punishing criminals. When she shared that with Malik, he became convinced that he would be the next victim. His misdemeanours may be minor, but that didn't seem to matter to the killer.

Sajan Malik began coordinating with Tengku, even following Summers to his mother-in-law's home. He watched Summers enter with two large boxes and leave without them. Curious what was in them, Malik took it upon himself to investigate and broke into her flat.

That had led to his arrest.

He was now petrified that Danny Summers would extract his revenge. He was so scared that he pleaded to meet Tengku in real life so she could protect him. Meanwhile, Tengku's surveillance had uncovered Danny's affair, although the identity of the woman was a mystery to her. It was during one such reconnaissance evening that Tengku missed her appointment with Malik. Their phones, both loaded with unregistered pre-paid sims, show a volley of text messages in which Malik pleaded to meet her that night. They'd arranged to do so near the industrial estate.

That was the night Malik was murdered.

Unbeknownst to them, Jack Weaver had become aware of Patricia's infidelity, but Danny's Summers' identity remained out of his reach. The only lead he had was Patricia, and by watching her, he came across Jenny Tengku. That night he followed Tengku when she met with Malik near the industrial park. He watched as photos were exchanged via their mobiles, then Tengku left. From his own notes, he couldn't believe this feeble Indian man was sleeping with Patricia, but why else was Tengku talking with him? When she left, Weaver moved in for the kill, fuelled by raw jealousy. From the rough notes in Weaver's journal, the two scuffled outside. The more powerful man ripping at his clothes and shoes, intending to strip him naked and punish him outside. But the little ferret had slipped his grasp and hid inside the warehouse.

It was only after he watched the fire team's body cam footage did he see that Jenny Tengku had returned to the scene of the crime, which made him think she may never have left it. As Garrick had become involved in the case, Weaver couldn't risk Tengku revealing what she knew, but he still didn't know who she was or where she lived.

Luckily, the police solved that mystery for him.

Only when breaking into her caravan did he discover the pictures of Danny Summers with Patricia. He may have killed the wrong man, but he now had to get rid of Tengku. He threw in the Selman incident as a red herring, hoping the police would think it was a circular closed case.

The entire incident gave Garrick a headache. Fanta had drawn the various timelines on the evidence wall so that the team had a clear visual representation to guide them, but with everybody in the saga dead, many truths would never be known. Such as Patricia Royston's real involvement in the killings. In Weaver's handwritten journals he had talked about how happy he was that she shared his passion for fire, but whether this was conversational, actual arson attacks, or even the killings, he'd left the details vague.

There was every chance she would get away with murder.

It was deeply frustrating, and Garrick had to remind

himself that not every case was perfectly tied with a bow. In fact, very few were.

This was reenforced the previous evening as the team left the station. Molly Meyers had been with them and talked to Garrick as he waited for Wendy to arrive to give him a lift home. She wanted to talk to him the following week about his sister. Nothing urgent, but she had identified a few more irregularities in the evidence. They had agreed to meet one day for lunch. She had given no hint about what was amiss, and he didn't have the mental bandwidth to find out.

Garrick drew his attention back to the moment. His feet were aching. There was very little in the way of conversation during the rest of the hike. The red-headed Sonia was just in front of them, but she was usually silent, and made no exception tonight. When everybody stopped at the pre-arranged pub for dinner and a much-needed break, even the diehard ramblers were quiet. Garrick had dreaded to find the motor-mouthed Duncan Cook sit next to him, but other than muttering a few words, exhaustion was keeping him quiet. Larry, the largest of the group and seemingly most unfit, was the only one talking as usual and showing no signs of tiredness. Judith sat next to Wendy, and they quietly talked, but Wendy was unusually reserved giving her answers.

Despite his fatigue, Garrick couldn't finish his Mac 'n' Cheese and skipped dessert. Wendy polished off her food in silence. Garrick pretended not to notice her sidelong glances, but the sense that she wanted to speak her mind was growing by the minute.

When they left the pub, it was dark. The temperature had plummeted, but the cold was the invigoration that Garrick needed to keep him focused. They all wore reflective jackets and head-torches and stayed together for the first fifteen minutes. After that, the different paces stretched the herd, until once again Garrick and Wendy found themselves lingering at the back.

An hour later, Wendy could no longer hold her thoughts hostage. Garrick felt her gloved hand scoop his and squeeze hard.

"I'm sorry I haven't been myself." Every time she looked at him, he was blinded by her head-torch. "But the last week has been... mad."

When Garrick tried to speak, he found his lips were dry. He licked them like a lizard just to get the words out. "I told you dating a copper wasn't straightforward." The words choked in his throat. He didn't want it to end, certainly not on a poxy night-time hike. After weeks of convalescing, they'd had plenty of time to enjoy each other and grow close. The last few weeks of intense work had undone it all. "I don't want to say goodbye..."

The last words came out in a combination of a feeble croak and a teenage plea. In one sentence, he'd embarrassed himself more than the last two decades combined. Wendy's hand released his, and she stopped in her tracks. He took several steps before realising and stopped as he turned to face her.

"What are you talking about?"

Garrick raised his hand to block her headlight, but it didn't help him see her face.

"I know work has been consuming me and you're going through a tough time quitting your job. But–"

"David Garrick, you are a complete dickhead."

That much he knew, but he was surprised that she was sniggering about it.

"You're right. This last week has changed us completely."

"I know. I'm sorry."

"Because I'm pregnant! You're going to be a dad!"

The blinding light meant that Garrick couldn't see her expression, and he hoped the same was true for her. He felt as if she'd physically slapped him across the face, while at the same time, tears streamed down his numb cheeks.

Life *was* about to change.

It was about to change in more ways than he could have possibly known.

ALSO BY M.G. COLE

info@mgcole.com

or say hello on Twitter: @mgcolebooks

SLAUGHTER OF INNOCENTS

DCI Garrick 1

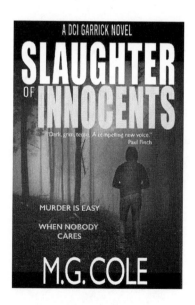

MURDER IS SKIN DEEP

DCI Garrick 2

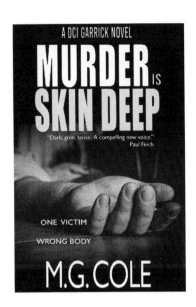

THE DEAD WILL TALK

DCI Garrick 3

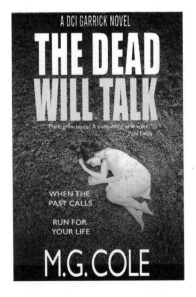

DEAD MAN'S GAME

DCI Garrick 4

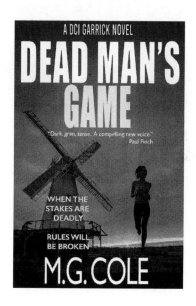

THE DEAD DON'T PAY

DCI Garrick 6 - COMING SOON!

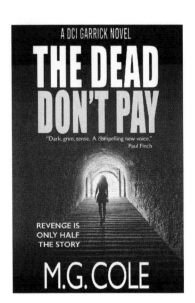

Printed in Great Britain
by Amazon

12405167R00142